The Branding Iron

"WILL YOU BE COMIN' HOME WITH ME, GEL?" (*page* 16)

The Branding Iron

By

Katharine Newlin Burt

WITH ILLUSTRATIONS

Fredonia Books
Amsterdam, The Netherlands

The Branding Iron

by
Katharine Newlin Burt

ISBN: 1-4101-0083-9

Reprinted from the 1919 edition

Fredonia Books
Amsterdam, The Netherlands
http://www.fredoniabooks.com

In order to make original editions of historical works available to scholars at an economical price, this facsimile of the original edition of 1919 is reproduced from the best available copy and has been digitally enhanced to improve legibility, but the text remains unaltered to retain historical authenticity.

Contents

Book One

THE TWO-BAR BRAND

Book Two

THE ESTRAY

Contents

Illustrations

From drawings by Charles Sarka

The Branding Iron

Book One

THE TWO-BAR BRAND

The Branding Iron

BOOK ONE: *The Two-Bar Brand*

CHAPTER I

JOAN READS BY FIRELIGHT

THERE is no silence so fearful, so breathless, so searching as the night silence of a wild country buried five feet deep in snow. For thirty miles or so, north, south, east, and west of the small, half-smothered speck of gold in Pierre Landis's cabin window, there lay, on a certain December night, this silence, bathed in moonlight. The cold was intense: below the bench where Pierre's homestead lay, there rose from the twisted, rapid river, a cloud of steam, above which the hoar-frosted tops of cottonwood trees were perfectly distinct, trunk, branch, and twig, against a sky the color of iris petals. The stars flared brilliantly, hardly dimmed by the full moon, and over the vast surface of the snow minute crystals kept up a steady shining of their own. The range of sharp, wind-scraped mountains, uplifted fourteen thousand feet, rode across the country, northeast, southwest, dazzling in white armor, spears up to the sky, a sight, seen suddenly, to take the breath, like the crashing march of archangels militant.

In the center of this ring of silent crystal, Pierre Landis's logs shut in a little square of warm and ruddy human darkness. Joan, his wife, made the heart of this defiant space — Joan, the one mind living in this ghostly area of night. She had put out the lamp, for Pierre, starting townward two days before, had warned her with a certain threatening sharpness not to waste oil, and she lay on the hearth, her rough head almost in the ashes, reading a book by the unsteady light of the flames. She followed the printed lines with a strong, dark forefinger and her lips framed the words with slow, whispering motions. It was a long, strong woman's body stretched there across the floor, heavily if not sluggishly built, dressed rudely in warm stuffs and clumsy boots, and it was a heavy face, too, unlit from within, but built on lines of perfect animal beauty. The head and throat had the massive look of a marble fragment stained to one even tone and dug up from Attic earth. And she was reading thus heavily and slowly, by firelight in the midst of this tremendous Northern night, Keats's version of Boccaccio's "Tale of Isabella and the Pot of Basil."

The story for some reason interested her. She felt that she could understand the love of young Lorenzo and of Isabella, the hatred of those two brothers and Isabella's horrible tenderness for that young murdered head. There were even things in her own life that she compared with these; in fact, at every phrase, she stopped, and, staring ahead, crudely and ignorantly visualized, after her own experience, what she had just read; and, in doing so, she pictured her own life.

Her love and Pierre's — her life before Pierre came — to put herself in Isabella's place, she felt back to the days before her love, when she had lived in a desolation of bleak poverty, up and away along Lone River in her father's shack. This log house of Pierre's was a castle by contrast. John Carver and his daughter had shared one room between them; Joan's bed curtained off with gunny-sacking in a corner. She slept on hides and rolled herself up in old dingy patchwork quilts and worn blankets. On winter mornings she would wake covered with the snow that had sifted in between the ill-matched logs. There had been a stove, one leg gone and substituted for by a huge cobblestone; there had been two chairs, a long box, a table, shelves — all rudely made by John; there had been guns and traps and snowshoes, hides, skins, the wings of birds, a couple of fishing-rods — John made his living by legal and illegal trapping and killing. He had looked like a trapped or hunted creature himself, small, furtive, very dark, with long fingers always working over his mouth, a great crooked nose — a hideous man, surely a hideous father. He hardly ever spoke, but sometimes, coming home from the town which he visited several times a year, but to which he had never taken Joan, he would sit down over the stove and go over heavily, for Joan's benefit, the story of his crime and his escape.

Joan always told herself that she would not listen, whatever he said she would stop her ears, but always the story fascinated her, held her, eyes widened on the figure by the stove. He had sat huddled in his chair, gnomelike, his face contorting with the emotions of the story, his own brilliant eyes fixed on the round, red mouth of the stove. The reflection of this scarlet circle was hideously noticeable in his pupils.

"A man's a right to kill his woman if she ain't honest with him," so the story began; "if he finds out she's ben trickin' of him, playin' him off fer another man. That was yer mother, gel; she was a bad woman." There followed a coarse and vivid description of her badness and the manner of it. "That kinder thing no man can let pass by in his wife. I found her" — again the rude details of his discovery — "an' I found him, an' I let him go fer the white-livered coward he was, but her I killed. I shot her dead after she'd said her prayers an' asked God's mercy on her soul. Then I walked off, but they kotched me an' I was tried. They did n't swing me. Out in them parts they knowed I was in my rights; so the boys held, but 't was a life sentence. They tuk me by rail down to Dawson an' I give 'em the slip, handcuffs an' all. Perhaps 't was only a half-hearted chase they made fer me. Some of them fellers mebbe had wives of their own." He always stopped to laugh at this point. "An' I cut off up country till I come to a smithy at the edge of a town. I hung round fer a spell till the smith hed gone off an' I got into his place an' rid me of the handcuffs. 'T was a job, but I was n't kotched at it an' I made myself free." Followed the story of his wanderings and his hardships and his coming to Lone River and setting out his traps. "In them days there were n't no law ag'in' trappin' beaver. A man could make a honest livin'. Now they 've tuk an' made laws ag'in' a man's bread an' butter. I ask ye, if 't ain't wrong on a Tuesday to trap yer beaver, why, 't ain't wrong the follerin' Tuesday. I don't see it, jes becos some fellers back there has made a law ag'in' it to suit theirselves. Anyway, the market fer beaver hides is still prime. Mebbe I'll leave you a fortin, gel. I've saved you from badness, anyhow. I risked a lot to go back an' git you, but I done it. You was playin' out in front of yer aunt's house an' I come fer you. You was a three-year-old an' a big youngster. Says I, 'What's yer name?' Says you, 'Joan Carver'; an' I knowed you by yer likeness to *her*. By God! I swore I'd save ye. I tuk you off with me, though you put up a fight an' I hed to use you rough to silence you. 'There ain't a-goin' to be no man in yer life, Joan Carver,' says I; 'you an' yer big eyes is a-goin' to be fer me, to do my work an' to look after my comforts. No pretty boys fer you an' no husbands either to go a-shootin' of you down fer yer sins.'" He shivered and shook his head. "No, here you stays with yer father an' grows up a good gel. There ain't a-goin' to be no man in *yer* life, Joan."

But youth was stronger than the man's half-crazy will, and when she was seventeen, Joan ran away.

She found her way easily enough to the town, for she was wise in the tracks of a wild country, and John's trail townwards, though so rarely used, was to her eyes plain enough; and very coolly she walked into the hotel, past the group of loungers around the stove, and asked at the desk, where Mrs. Upper sat, if she could get a job. Mrs. Upper and the loungers stared, for there were few women in this frontier country and those few were well known. This great, strong girl, heavily graceful in her heavily awkward clothes, bareheaded, shod like a man, her face and throat purely classic, her eyes gray and wide and as secret in expression as an untamed beast's — no one had ever seen the like of her before.

"What's yer name?" asked Mrs. Upper suspiciously. It was Mormon Day in the town; there were celebrations and her house was full; she needed extra hands, but where this wild creature was concerned she was doubtful.

"Joan. I'm John Carver's daughter," answered the girl.

At once comprehension dawned; heads were nodded, then craned for a better look. Yes, the town, the whole country even, had heard of John Carver's imprisoned daughter. Sober and drunk, he had boasted of her and of how there was to be "no man" in her life. It was like dangling ripe fruit above the mouths of hungry boys to make such a boast in such a land. But they were lazy. It was a country of lazy, slow-thinking, slow-moving, and slow-talking adventurers — you will notice this ponderous, inevitable quality of rolling stones — and though men talked with humor not too fine of "travelin' up Lone River for John's gel," not a man had got there. Perhaps the men knew John Carver for a coward, that most dangerous animal to meet in his own lair.

Now here stood the "gel," the mysterious secret goal of desire, a splendid creature, virginal, savage, as certainly designed for man as Eve. The men's eyes fastened upon her, moved and dropped.

"Your father sent you down here fer a job?" asked Mrs. Upper incredulously.

"No. I come." Joan's grave gaze was unchanging. "I'm tired of it up there. I ain't a-goin' back. I'm most eighteen now an' I kinder want a change."

She had not meant to be funny, but a gust of laughter rattled the room. She shrank back. It was more terrifying to her than any cruelty she had fancied meeting her in the town. These were the men her father had forbidden, these loud-laughing, crinkled faces. She had turned to brave them, a great surge of color in her brows.

"Don't mind the boys, dear," spoke Mrs. Upper. "They will laff, joke or none. We ain't none of us blamin' you. It's a wonder you ain't run off long afore now. I can give you a job an' welcome, but you'll be green an' unhandy. Well, sir, we kin learn ye. You kin turn yer hand to chamber-work an' mebbe help at the table. Maud will show you. But, Joan, what will dad do to you? He'll be takin' after you hot-foot, I reckon, an' be fer gettin' you back home as soon as he can."

Joan did not change her look.

"I'll not be goin' back with him," she said.

Her slow, deep voice, chest notes of a musical vibration, stirred the room. The men were hers and gruffly said so. A sudden warmth enveloped her from heart to foot. She followed Mrs. Upper to the initiation in her service, clothed for the first time in human sympathies.

CHAPTER II

PIERRE LAYS HIS HAND ON A HEART

MAUD UPPER was the first girl of her own age that Joan had ever seen. Joan went in terror of her and Maud knew this and enjoyed her ascendancy over an untamed creature twice her size. There was the crack of a lion-tamer's whip in the tone of her instructions. That was after a day or two. At first Maud had been horribly afraid of Joan. "A wild thing like her, livin' off there in the hills with that man, why, ma, there's no tellin' what she might be doin' to me."

"She won't hurt ye," laughed Mrs. Upper, who had lived in the wilds herself, having been a frontierman's wife before the days even of this frontier town and having married the hotel-keeper as a second venture. She knew that civilization — this rude place being civilization to Joan — would cow the girl and she knew that Maud's self-assertive buoyancy would frighten the soul of her. Maud was large-hipped, high-bosomed, with a small, round waist much compressed. She carried her head, with its waved brown hair, very high, and shot blue glances down along a short, broad nose. Her mouth was thin and determined, her color high. She had a curiously shallow, weak voice that sounded breathless. She taught Joan impatiently and laughed loudly but not unkindly at her ways.

"Gee, she's awkward, ain't she?" she would say to the men; "trail like a bull moose!"

The men grinned, but their eyes followed Joan's movements. As a matter of fact, she was not awkward. Through her clumsy clothes, the heaviness of her early youth, in spite of all the fetters of her ignorance, her wonderful long bones and her wonderful strength asserted themselves. And she never hurried. At first this apparent sluggishness infuriated Maud. "Get a gait on ye, Joan Carver!" she would scream above the din of the rough meals, but soon she found that Joan's slow movements accomplished a tremendous amount of work in an amazingly short time. There was no pause in the girl's activity. She poured out her strength as a python pours his, noiselessly, evenly, steadily, no haste, no waste. And the men's eyes brooded upon her.

If Joan had stayed long at Mrs. Upper's, she would have begun inevitably to model herself on Maud, who was, in her eyes, a marvelous thing of beauty. But, just a week after her arrival, there came to the inn Pierre Landis and for Joan began the strange and terrible history of love.

In the lives of most women, of the vast majority, the clatter and clash of housewifery prelude and postlude the spring song of their years. And the rattle of dishes, of busy knives and forks, the quick tapping of Maud's attendant feet, the sound of young and ravenous jaws at work: these sounds were in Joan's bewildered ears, and the sights which they accompanied in her bewildered eyes, just before she heard Pierre's voice, just before she saw his face.

It was dinner hour at the hotel, an hour most dreadful to Joan because of the hurry, the strangeness, and the crowd, because of the responsibility of her work, but chiefly because at that hour she expected the appearance of her father. Her eyes were often on the door. It opened to admit the young men, the riders and ranchers who hung up their hats, swaggered with a little jingle of spurs to their chairs; clean-faced, clean-handed, wet-haired, murmuring low-voiced courtesies, — "Pass me the gravy, please," "I would n't be carin' fer any, thank you," — and lifting to the faces of waiting girls now and again their strange, young, brooding eyes, bold, laughing, and afraid, hungry, pathetic, arrogant, as the eyes of young men are, tameless and untamable, but full of the pathos of the untamed. Joan's heart shook a little under their looks, but when Pierre lifted his eyes to her, her heart stood still. She had not seen them following her progress around the room. He had come in late, and finding no place at the long, central table sat apart at a smaller one under a high, uncurtained window. By the time she met his eyes they were charged with light; smoky-blue eyes they were, the iris heavily ringed with black, the pupils dilated a little. For the first time it occurred to Joan, looking down with a still heart into his eyes, that a man might be beautiful. The blood came up from her heart to her face. Her eyes struggled away from his.

"What's yer name, gel?" murmured Pierre.

"Joan Carver."

"You run away from home?" He too had heard of her.

"Yes."

"Will your father be takin' you back?"

"I won't be goin' with him."

She was about to pass on. Pierre cast a swift look about the table — bent heads and busy hands, eyes cast down, ears, he knew, alert. It was a land of few women and of many men.

He must leave in the morning early and for months he would not be back. He put out a long, hard hand, caught Joan's wrist and gave it a queer, urgent shake, the gesture of an impatient and beseeching child.

"Will you be comin' home with me, gel?" asked Pierre hurriedly.

She looked at him, her lips apart, and she shook her head.

Maud's voice screamed at her from the kitchen door. Pierre let her go. She went on, very white.

She did not sleep at all that night. Her father's face, Pierre's face, looked at her. In the morning Pierre would be gone. She had heard Maud say that the "queer Landis feller would be makin' tracks back to that ranch of his acrost the river." Yes, he would be gone. She might have been going with him. She felt the urgent pressure of his hand on her arm, in her heart. It shook her with such a longing for love, for all the unknown largesse of love, that she cried. The next morning, pale, she came down and went about her work. Pierre was not at breakfast, and she felt a sinking of heart, though she had not known that she had built upon seeing him again. Then, as she stepped out at the back to empty a bucket, there he was!

Not even the beauty of dawn could lend mystery to the hideous, littered yard, untidy as the yards of frontier towns invariably are, to the board fence, to the trampled half-acre of dirt, known as "The Square," and to the ugly frame buildings straggled about it; but it could and did give an unearthly look of blessedness to the bare, gray-brown buttes that ringed the town and a glory to the sky, while upon Pierre, waiting at his pony's head, it shed a magical and tender light. He was dressed in his cowboy's best, a white silk handkerchief knotted under his chin, leather "chaps," bright spurs, a sombrero on his head. His face was grave, excited, wistful. At sight of Joan, he moved forward, the pony trailing after him at the full length of its reins; and, stopping before her, Pierre took off the sombrero, slowly stripped the gauntlet from his right hand, and, pressing both hat and glove against his hip with the left hand, held out the free, clean palm to Joan.

"Good-bye," said he, "unless — you'll be comin' with me after all?"

Joan felt again that rush of fire to her brows. She took his hand and her fingers closed around it like the frightened, lonely fingers of a little girl. She came near to him and looked up.

"I'll be comin' with you, Pierre," she said, just above her breath.

He shot up a full inch, stiffened, searched her with smouldering eyes, then held her hard against him. "You'll not be sorry, Joan Carver," said he gently and put her away from him. Then, unsmiling, he bade her go in and get her belongings while he got her a horse and told his news to Mrs. Upper.

That ride was dreamlike to Joan. Pierre put her in her saddle and she rode after him across the Square and along a road flanked by the ugly houses of the town.

"Where are we a-goin'?" she asked him timidly.

He stopped at that, turned, and, resting his hand on the cantle of his saddle, smiled at her for the first time.

"Don't you savvy the answer to that question, Joan?"

She shook her head.

The smile faded. "We're goin' to be married," said he sternly, and they rode on.

They were married by the justice, a pleasant, silent fellow, who with Western courtesy, asked no more questions than were absolutely needful, and in fifteen minutes Joan mounted her horse again, a ring on the third finger of her left hand.

"Now," said Pierre, standing at her stirrup, his shining, smoke-blue eyes lifted to her, his hand on her boot, "you'll be wantin' some things — some clothes?"

"No," said Joan. "Maud went with me an' helped me buy things with my pay just yesterday. I won't be needin' anything."

"All right," said he. "We're off, then!" And he flung himself with a sudden wild, boyish "Whoopee!" on his pony, gave a clip to Joan's horse and his own, and away they galloped, a pair of young, wild things, out from the town through a straggling street to where the road boldly stretched itself toward a great land of sagebrush, of buttes humping their backs against the brilliant sky. Down the valley they rode, trotting, walking, galloping, till, turning westward, they mounted a sharp slope and came up above the plain. Below, in the heart of the long, narrow valley, the river coiled and wandered, divided and came together again into a swift stream, amongst aspen islands and willow swamps. Beyond this strange, lonely river-bed, the cottonwoods began, and, above them, the pine forests massed themselves and strode up the foothills of the gigantic range, that range of iron rocks, sharp, thin, and brittle where they scraped the sky.

At the top of the hill, Pierre put out his hand and pulled Joan's rein, drawing her to a stop beside him.

"Over yonder's my ranch," said he.

Joan looked. There was not a sign of house or clearing, but she followed his gesture and nodded.

"Under the mountains?" she said.

"At the foot of Thunder Cañon. You can see a gap in the pines. There's a waterfall just above — that white streak. Now you've got it. Where you come from's to the south, away yonder."

Joan would not turn her head. "Yes," said she, "I know."

Suddenly tears rushed to her eyes. She had a moment of unbearable longing and regret. Pierre said nothing; he was not watching her.

"Come on," said he, "or your father will be takin' after us."

They rode at a gallop down the hill.

CHAPTER III

TWO PICTURES IN THE FIRE

THE period which followed had a quality of breathless, almost unearthly happiness. They were young, savage, simple, and their love, unanalyzed, was as joyous as the loves of animals: joyous with that clear gravity characteristic of the boy and girl. Pierre had been terribly alone before Joan came, and the building-up of his ranch had occupied his mind day and night except, now and again, for dreams. Yet he was of a passionate nature. Joan felt in him sometimes a savage possibility of violence. Two incidents of this time blazed themselves especially on her memory: the one, her father's visit, the other, an irrelevant enough picture until after events threw back a glare upon it.

They had been at Pierre's ranch for a fortnight before John Carver found them. Then, one morning, as Pierre opened the door to go out to work, Joan saw a thin, red pony tied to the fence and a small figure walking toward the cabin.

"Pierre, it's father!" she said. And Pierre

stopped in his tracks, drew himself up and waited, hands on his cartridge belt.

How mean and old and furtive her father looked in contrast to this beautiful young husband! Joan was entirely unafraid. She leaned against the side of the door and watched, as silent and unconsulted as any squaw, while the two men settled their property rights in her.

"So you've took my gel," said John Carver, stopping a foot or two in front of Pierre, his eyes shifting up and down, one long hand fingering his lips.

Pierre answered courteously. "Some man was bound to hev her, Mr. Carver, soon or late. You can't set your face ag'in' the laws of natur'. Will you be steppin' in? Joan will give you some breakfast."

Carver paid no heed to the invitation. "Hev you married her?" said he.

The blood rose to Pierre's brown face. "Sure I hev."

"Well, sir, you hev married the darter of a ——" Carver used a brutal word. "Look out fer her. If you see her eyes lookin' an' lookin' at another man, you kin know what's to come." Pierre was white. "I've done with her. She kin never come to me fer bite or bed. Shoot her if you hev to, Pierre Landis, but when she's kotched at her mother's game, don't send her back to me. That's all I come to say."

He turned with limber agility and went back to his horse. He was on it and off, galloping madly across the sagebrush flat. Pierre turned and walked into the house past Joan without a word.

She still leaned against the door, but her head was bent.

Presently she went about her housework. Every now and then she shot a wistful look at Pierre. All morning long, he sat there, his hands hanging between his knees, his eyes full of a brooding trouble. At noon he shook his head, got up, and, still without word or caress, he strode out and did not come back till dark. Joan suffered heartache and terror. When he came, she ran into his arms. He kissed her, seemed quite himself again, and the strange interview was never mentioned by either of them. They were silent people, given to feelings and to action rather than to thoughts and words.

The other memory was of a certain sunset hour when she came at Pierre's call out to the shed he had built at one side of their cabin. Its open side faced the west, and, as Joan came, her shadow went before her and fell across Pierre at work. The flame of the west gave a weird pallor to the flames over which he bent. He was whistling, and hammering at a long piece of iron. Joan came and stood beside him.

Suddenly he straightened up and held in the air a bar of metal, the shaped end white hot. Joan blinked.

"That's our brand, gel," said Pierre. "Don't you fergit it. When I've made my fortune there'll be stock all over the country marked with them two bars. That'll be famous — the Two-Bar Brand. Don't you fergit it, Joan."

And he brought the white iron close so that she felt its heat on her face and drew back, flinching. He laughed, let it fall, and kissed her. Joan was very glad and proud.

CHAPTER IV

THE SIN-BUSTER

IN the fall, when the whole country had turned to a great cup of gold, purple-rimmed under the sky, Pierre went out into the hills after his winter meat. Joan was left alone. She spent her time cleaning and arranging the two-room cabin, and tidying up outdoors, and in "grubbing sage-brush," a gigantic task, for the one hundred and fifty acres of Pierre's homestead were covered for the most part by the sturdy, spicy growth, and every bush had to be dug out and burnt to clear the way for ploughing and planting. Joan worked with the deliberateness and intentness of a man. She enjoyed the wholesome drudgery. She was proud every sundown of the little clearing she had made, and stood, tired and content, to watch the piled brush burn, sending up aromatic smoke and curious, dull flames very high into the still air.

She was so standing, hands folded on her rake, when, on the other side of her conflagration, she perceived a man. He was steadily regarding her, and when her eyes fell upon him, he smiled and stepped forward — a tall, broad, very fair young man in a shooting coat, khaki riding-breeches, and puttees. He had a wide brow, clear, blue eyes and an eager, sensitive, clean-shaven mouth and chin. He held out a big white hand.

"Mrs. Landis," he said, in a crisp voice of an accent and finish strange to the girl "I wonder if you and your husband can put me up for the night. I'm Frank Holliwell. I'm on a round of parish visits, and, as my parish is about sixty miles square, my poor old pony has gone lame. I know you are not my parishioners, though, no doubt, you should be, but I'm going to lay claim to your hospitality, for all that, if I may?"

Joan had moved her rake into the grasp of her left hand and had taken the proffered palm into her other, all warm and fragrantly stained.

"You're the new sin-buster, ain't you?" she asked gravely.

The young man opened his blue and friendly eyes.

"Oh, that's what I am, eh? That's a new one to me. Yes. I suppose I am. It's rather a fine name to go by — sin-buster," and he laughed very low and very amusedly.

Joan looked him over and slowly smiled. "You look like you could bust anything you'd a mind to," she said, and led the way toward the house, her rake across her shoulder.

"Pierre," she told him when they were in the shining, clean log house, "is off in the hills after his elk, but I can make you up a bed in the settin'-room an' serve you a supper an' welcome."

"Oh, thanks," he rather doubtfully accepted.

Evidently he did not know the ways and proprieties of this new "parish" of his. But Joan seemed to take the situation with an enormous calm impersonality. He modeled his manner upon hers. They sat at the table together, Joan silent, save when he forced her to speak, and entirely untroubled by her silence, Frank Holliwell eating heartily, helping her serve, and talking a great deal. He asked her a great many questions, which she answered with direct simplicity. By the end of dish-washing, he had her history and more of her opinions, probably, than any other creature she had met.

"What do you do when Landis is away?"

She told him.

"But, in the evenings, I mean, after work. Have you books?"

"No," said Joan; "it's right hard labor, readin'. Pa learned me my letters an' I can spell out bits from papers an' advertisements an' what not, but I ain't never read a book straight out. I dunno," she added presently, "but as I'd like to. Pierre can read," she told him proudly.

"I'm sure you'd like to." He considered her through the smoke of his pipe. He was sitting by the hearth now, and she, just through with clearing up, stood by the corner of the mantel shelf, arranging the logs. The firelight danced over her face, so beautiful, so unlighted from within.

"How old are you, Joan Landis?" he asked suddenly, using her name without title for the first time.

"Eighteen."

"Is that all? You must read books, you know. There's so much empty space there back of your brows."

She looked up smiling a little, her wide gray eyes puzzled.

"Yes, Joan. You must read. Will you — if I lend you some books?"

She considered. "Yes," she said. "I'd read them if you'd be lendin' me some. In the evenings when Pierre's away, I'm right lonesome. I never was lonesome before, not to know it. It'll take me a long time to read one book, though," she added with an engaging mournfulness.

"What do you like — stories, poetry, magazines?"

"I'd like real books in stiff covers," said Joan, "an' I don't like pictures."

This surprised the clergyman. "Why not?" said he.

"I like to notion how the folks look myself. I like pictures of real places, that has got to be like they are" — Joan was talking a great deal and having trouble with her few simple words — "but I like folks in stories to look like I want 'em to look."

"Not the way the writer describes them?"

"Yes, sir. But you can make up a whole lot on what the writer describes. If he says 'her eyes is blue'; you can see 'em dark blue or light blue or jest blue. An' you can see 'em shaped round or what not, the way you think about folks that you've heard of an' have never met."

It was extraordinary how this effort at self-expression excited Joan. She was rarely self-conscious, but she was usually passive or stolid; now there was a brilliant flush in her face and her large eyes deepened and glowed. "I heerd tell of you, Mr. Holliwell. Fellers come up here to see Pierre onct in a while an' one or two of 'em spoke your name. An' I kinder figured out you was a weedy feller, awful solemn-like, an' of course you ain't, but it's real hard for me to notion that there ain't two Mr. Holliwells, you an' the weedy sin-buster I've ben picturin'. Like as not I'll get to thinkin' of you like two fellers." Joan sighed. "Seems like when I onct get a notion in my head it jest sticks there some way."

"Then the more wise notions you get the better. I'll ride up here in a couple of weeks' time with some books. You may keep them as long as you will. All winter, if you like. When I can get up here, we can talk them over, you and Landis and I. I'll try to choose some without pictures. There will be stories and some poetry, too."

"I ain't never read but one pome," said Joan.

"And that was?"

She had sat down on the floor by the hearth, her head thrown back to lean against the cobbles of the chimney-piece, her knees locked in her hands. That magnificent long throat of hers ran up to the black coils of hair which had slipped heavily down over her ears. The light edged her round chin and her strongly modeled, regular features; the full, firm mouth so savagely pure and sensuous and self-contained. The eyes were mysterious under their thick lashes and dark, long brows. This throat and face and these strong hands were picked out in their full value of line and texture from the dark cotton dress she was wearing.

"It's a pome on a card what father had, stuck ag'in' the wall." She began to recite, her eyes fixed upon him with childlike gravity. "'He maketh me to lie down in green pastures: He leadeth me beside the still waters. . . . Yea, though I walk through the valley of shadows, thou art with me, thy rod and thy staff they comfort me.'"

Holliwell had taken the pipe from between his teeth, had straightened up. Her deep voice, the slight swinging of her body to the rhythm she had unconsciously given to her lines, the strange glow in her eyes . . . Holliwell wondered why these things, this brief, sing-song recitation, had given a light thrill to the surface of his skin, had sent a tingling to his finger-tips. He was the first person to wonder at that effect of Joan's cadenced music. "The valley of the shadow —" she had missed a familiar phrase and added value to a too often repeated line.

"Joan! Joan!" said the "sin-buster," an exclamation drawn from him on a deep breath, "what an extraordinary girl you are! What a marvelous woman you are going to be!"

Joan looked at him in a silence of pure astonishment and that was the end of their real talk.

CHAPTER V

PIERRE BECOMES ALARMED ABOUT HIS PROPERTY

THE next time Holliwell came, he brought the books, and, finding Pierre at home, he sat with his host after supper and talked men's talk of the country; of game, of ranching, a little gossip, stories of travel, humorous experiences, and Joan sat in her place, the books in her lap, looking and listening.

John Carver had used a phrase, "When you see her eyes lookin' and lookin' at another man —" and this phrase had stuck in Pierre's sensitive and jealous memory. What Joan felt for Holliwell was a sort of ignorant and respectful tenderness, the excitement of an intelligent child first moved to a knowledge of its own intelligence; the gratitude of savage loneliness toward the beautiful feet of exploration. A consciousness of her clean mind, a consciousness of her young, untamed spirit, had come slowly to life in her since her talk with Holliwell. Joan was peculiarly a woman — that is, the passive and receptive being. Pierre had laid his hand on her heart and she had followed him; now this young parson had put a curious finger on her brain, it followed him. Her husband saw the admiration, the gratitude, the tender excitement in her frank eyes, and the poison seed sown by John Carver's hand shot out roots and tiny, deadly branches.

But Joan and Holliwell were unaware. Pierre smoked rapidly, rolling cigarette after cigarette; he listened with a courteous air, he told stories in his soft, slow voice; once he went out to bring in a fresh log and, coming back on noiseless feet, saw Joan and her instructor bent over one of the books and Joan's face was almost that of a stranger, so eager, so flushed, with sparkles in the usually still, gray eyes.

It was not till a week or two after this second visit from the clergyman that Pierre's smouldering jealousy broke into flame. After clearing away the supper things with an absent air of eager expectation, Joan would dry her hands on her apron, and, taking down one of her books from their place in a shelf corner, she would draw her chair close to the lamp and begin to read, forgetful of Pierre. These had been the happiest hours for him; he would tell Joan about his day's work, about his plans, about his past life; wonderful it was to him, after his loneliness, that she should be sitting there drinking in every word and loving him with her dumb, wild eyes. Now, there was no talk and no listening. Joan's absorbed face was turned from him and bent over her book, her lips moved, she would stop and stare before her. After a long while, he would get up and go to bed, but she would stay with her books till a restless movement from him would make her aware of the lamplight shining wakefulness upon him through the chinks in the partition wall. Then she would get up reluctantly, sighing, and come to bed.

For ten evenings this went on, Pierre's heart slowly heating itself, until, all at once, the flame leaped.

Joan had untied her apron and reached up for her book. Pierre had been waiting, hoping that of her free will she might prefer his company to the "parson feller's" — for in his ignorance those books were jealously personified — but, without a glance in his direction, she had turned as usual to the shelf.

"You goin' to read?" asked Pierre hoarsely. It was a painful effort to speak.

She turned with a childish look of astonishment. "Yes, Pierre."

He stood up with one of his lithe, swift movements, all in one rippling piece. "By God, you're not, though!" said he, strode over to her, snatched the volume from her, threw it back into its place, and pointed her to her chair.

"You set down an' give heed to me fer a change, Joan Carver," he said, his smoke-colored eyes smouldering. "I did n't fetch you up here to read parsons' books an' waste oil. I fetched you up here — to —" He stopped, choked with a sudden, enormous hurt tenderness and sat down and fell to smoking and staring, hot-eyed, into the fire.

And Joan sat silent in her place, puzzled, wistful, wounded, her idle hands folded, looking at him for a while, then absently before her, and he knew that her mind was busy again with the preacher feller's books. If he had known better how to explain his heart, if she had known how to show him the impersonal eagerness of her awakening mind —! But, savage and silent, they sat there, loving each other, hurt, but locked each into his own impenetrable life.

After that, Joan changed the hours of her study and neglected housework and sagebrush-grubbing, but, nonetheless, were Pierre's evenings spoiled. Perfection of intercourse is the most perishable of all life's commodities. Now, when he talked, he could not escape the consciousness of having constrained his audience; she could not escape her knowledge of his jealousy, the remembrance of his mysterious outbreak, the irrepressible tug of the story she was reading. So it went on till snow came and they were shut in, man and wife, with only each other to watch, a tremendous test of good-fellowship. This searching intimacy came at a bad time, just after Holliwell's third visit when he had brought a fresh supply of books.

"There's poetry this time," he said. "Get Pierre to read it aloud to you."

The suggestion was met by a rude laugh from Pierre.

"I would n't be wastin' my time," he jeered.

It was the first rift in his courtesy. Holliwell looked up in sharp surprise. He saw a flash of the truth, a little wriggle of the green serpent in Pierre's eyes before they fell. He flushed and glanced at Joan. She stood by the table in the circle of lamplight, looking over the new books, but in her eagerness there was less simplicity. She wore an almost timorous air, accepted his remarks in silence, shot doubtful looks at Pierre before she answered questions, was an entirely different Joan. Now Holliwell was angry and he stiffened toward his host and hostess, dropped all his talk about the books and smoked haughtily. He was young and over-sensitive, no more master of himself in this instance than Pierre and Joan. But before he left after supper, refusing a bed, though Pierre conquered his dislike sufficiently to urge it, Holliwell had a moment with Joan. It was very touching. He would tell about it afterwards, but, for a long time, he could not bear to remember it.

She tried to return his books, coming with her arms full of them and lifting up eyes that were almost tragic with renunciation.

"I can't be takin' the time to read them, Mr. Holliwell," she said, that extraordinary, over-expressive voice of hers running an octave of regret; "an' someway Pierre don't like that I should spend my evenin's on them. Seems like he thinks I was settin' myself up to be knowin' more than him." She laughed ruefully. "Me — knowin' more'n Pierre! It's laughable. But anyways I don't want him to be thinkin' that. So take the books, please. I like them." She paused. "I love them," she said hungrily and, blinking, thrust them into his hands.

He put them down on the table. "You're wrong, Joan," he said quickly. "You must n't give in to such a foolish idea. You have rights of your own, a life of your own. Pierre must n't stand in the way of your learning. You must n't let him. I'll speak to him."

"Oh, no!" Some intuition warned her of the danger in his doing this.

"Well, then, keep your books and talk to Pierre about them. Try to persuade him to read aloud to you. I shan't be back now till spring, but I want you to read this winter, read all the stuff that's there. Come, Joan, to please me," and he smiled coaxingly.

"I ain't afeared of Pierre," said Joan slowly. Her pride was stung by the suggestion. "I'll keep the books." She sighed. "Good-bye. When I see you in the spring, I'll be a right learned school-marm."

She held out her hand and he took and held it, pressing it in his own. He felt troubled about her, unwilling to leave her in the snowbound wilderness with that young savage of the smouldering eyes.

"Good-bye," said Pierre behind him. His soft voice had a click.

Holliwell turned to him. "Good-bye, Landis. I shan't see either of you till the spring. I wish you a good winter and I hope —" He broke off and held out his hand. "Well," said he, "you're pretty far out of every one's way here. Be good to each other."

"Damn your interference!" said Pierre's eyes, but he took the hand and even escorted Holliwell to his horse.

Snow came early and deep that winter. It fell for long, gray days and nights, and then it came in hurricanes of drift, wrapping the cabin in swirling white till only one window peered out and one gabled corner cocked itself above the crust. Pierre had cut and stacked his winter wood; he had sent his cows to a richer man's ranch for winter feeding. There was very little for him to do. After he had brought in two buckets of water from the well and had cut, for the day's consumption, a piece of meat from his elk hanging outside against the wall, he had only to sit and smoke, to read old magazines and papers, and to watch Joan. Then the poisonous roots of his jealousy struck deep. Always his brain, unaccustomed to physical idleness, was at work, falsely interpreting her wistful silence — she was thinking of the parson, hungry to read his books, longing for the open season and his coming again to the ranch.

In December a man came in on snowshoes bringing "the mail" — one letter for Pierre, a communication which brought heat to his face. The Forest Service threatened him with a loss of land; it pointed to some flaw in his title; part of his property, the most valuable part, had not yet been surveyed. . . . Pierre looked up with set jaws, every fighting instinct sharpened to hold what was his own.

"I hev put in two years' hard work on them acres," he told his visitor, "an' I'm not plannin' to give them over to the first fool favored by the Service. My title is as clean as my hand. It'll take more'n thievery an' more'n spite to take it away from me."

"You better go to Robinson," advised the bearer of the letter; "can't get after them fellers too soon. It's a country where you can easy come by what you want, but where it ain't so easy to hold on to it. If it ain't yer land, it's yer hosses; if it ain't yer hosses, it's yer wife." He looked at Joan and laughed.

Pierre went white and dumb; the chance shot had inflamed his wound.

He strapped on his snowshoes and bade a grim good-bye to Joan, after the man had left. "Don't you be wastin' oil while I'm away," he told her sharply, standing in the doorway, his head level with the steep wall of snow behind him, and he gave her a threatening look so that the tenderness in her heart was frozen.

After he had gone, "Pierre, say a real good-bye, say good-bye," she whispered. Her face cramped and tears came.

She heard his steps lightly crunching across the hard, bright surface of the snow, they entered into the terrible frozen silence. Then she turned from the door, dried her eyes with her sleeve like a little village girl, and ran across the room to a certain shelf. Pierre would be gone a week. She would not waste oil, but she would read. It was with the appetite of a starved creature that she fell upon her books.

CHAPTER VI

PIERRE TAKES STEPS TO PRESERVE HIS PROPERTY

A LOG fell forward and Joan lifted her head. She had not come to an end of Isabella's tragedy nor of her own memories, but something other than the falling log had startled her; a light, crunching step upon the snow.

She looked toward the window. For an instant the room was almost dark and the white night peered in at her, its gigantic snow-peaks pressing against the long, horizontal window panes, and in that instant she saw a face. The fire started up again, the white night dropped away, the face shone close a moment longer, then it too disappeared. Joan came to her feet with pounding pulses. It had been Pierre's face, but at the same time, the face of a stranger. He had come back five days too soon and something terrible had happened. Surely his chancing to see her with her book would not make him look like that. Besides, she was not wasting oil. She had stood up, but at first she was incapable of moving forward. For the first time in her life she knew the paralysis of unreasoning fear. Then the door opened and Pierre came in out of the crystal night.

"What brought you back so soon?" asked Joan.

"Too soon fer you, eh?" He strode over to the hearth where she had lain, took up the book, struck it with his hand as though it had been a hated face, and flung it into the fire. "I seen you through the window," he said. "So you been happy readin' while I been away?"

"I'll get you supper. I'll light the lamp," Joan stammered.

Pierre's face was pale, his black hair lay in wet streaks on his temples. He must have traveled at furious speed through the bitter cold to be in such a sweat. There was a mysterious, controlled disorder in his look and there arose from him the odor of strong drink. But he was steady and sure in all his movements and his eyes were deadly cool and reasonable — only it was the reasonableness of insanity, reasonableness based on the wildest premises of unreason.

"I don't want no supper, nor no light," he said. "Firelight's enough fer you to read parsons' books by, it's enough fer me to do what I oughter done long afore to-night."

She stood in the middle of the small, log-walled

room, arrested in the act of lighting a match, and stared at him with troubled eyes. She was no longer afraid. After all, strange as he looked, more strangely as he talked, he was her Pierre, her man. The confidence of her heart had not been seriously shaken by his coldness and his moods during this winter. There had been times of fierce, possessive tenderness. She was his own woman, his property; at this low counting did she rate herself. A sane man does no injury to his own possessions. And Pierre, of course, was sane. He was tired, angry, he had been drinking — her ignorance, her inexperience led her to put little emphasis on the effects of the poison sold at the town saloon. When he was warm and fed and rested, he would be quite himself again. She went about preparing a meal in spite of his words.

He did not seem to notice this. He had taken his eyes from her at last and was busy with the fire. She, too, busy and reassured by the familiar occupation, ceased to watch him. Her pulses were quiet now. She was even beginning to be glad of his return. Why had she been so frightened? Of course, after such a terrible journey alone in the bitter cold, he would look strange. Her father, when he came back smelling of liquor, had always been more than usually morose and unlike his every-day self. He would sit over the stove and tell her the story of his crime. They were horrible home-comings, horrible evenings, but the next morning they would seem like dreams. To-morrow this strangeness of Pierre's would be mistlike and unreal.

"I seen your sin-buster in town," said Pierre. He was squatting on his heels over the fire which he had built up to a great blaze and glow and he spoke in a queer sing-song tone through his teeth. "He asked after you real kind. He wanted to know how you was gettin' on with the edication he's ben handin' out to you. I tell him that you was right satisfied with me an' my ways an' hed quit his books. I did n't know as you was hevin' such a good time durin' my absence."

Joan was cruelly hurt. His words seemed to fall heavily upon her heart. "I was n't hevin' a good time. I was missin' you, Pierre," said she in a low tremolo of grieving music. "Them books, they seemed like they was all the company I hed."

"You looked like you was missin' me," he sneered. "The sin-buster an' I had words about you, Joan. Yes'm, he give me quite a line of preachin' about you, Joan, as how you hed oughter develop yer own life in yer own way — along the lines laid out by him. I told him as how I knowed best what was right an' fittin' fer my own wife; as how, with a mother like your'n you needed watchin' more'n learnin'; as how you belonged to me an' not to him. An', says he, 'She don't belong to any man, Pierre Landis,' he said, 'neither to you nor to me. She belongs to her own self.' 'I'll see that she belongs to me,' I said. 'I'll fix her so she'll know it an' every other feller will.'"

At that he turned from the fire and straightened to his feet.

Joan moved backward slowly to the door. He had made no threatening sign or movement, but her fear had come overwhelmingly upon her and every instinct urged her to flight. But before she touched the handle of the door, he flung himself with deadly, swift force and silence across the room and took her in his arms. With all her wonderful young strength, Joan could not break away from him. He dragged her back to the hearth, tied her elbows behind her with the scarf from his neck, that very scarf he had worn when the dawn had shed a wistful beauty upon him, waiting for her on a morning not so very long ago. Joan went weak.

"Pierre," she cried pitifully, "what are you a-goin' to do to me?"

He roped her to the heavy post of a set of shelves built against the wall. Then he stood away, breathing fast.

"Now whose gel are you, Joan Carver?" he asked her.

"You know I'm yours, Pierre," she sobbed. "You got no need to tie me to make me say that."

"I got to tie you to make you do more'n say it. I got to make sure you are it. Hell-fire won't take the sureness out of me after this."

She turned her head, all that she could turn.

He was bending over the fire, and when he straightened she saw that he held something in his hand . . . a long bar of metal, white at the shaped end. At once her memory showed her a broad glow of sunset falling over Pierre at work. "There'll be stock all over the country marked with them two bars," he had said. "The Two-Bar Brand, don't you fergit it!" She was not likely to forget it now.

She shut her eyes. He stepped close to her and jerked her blouse down from her shoulder. She writhed away from him, silent in her rage and fear and fighting dumbly. She made no appeal. At that moment her heart was so full of hatred that it was hardened to pride. He lifted his brand and set it against the bare flesh of her shoulder.

Then terribly she screamed. Again, when he took the metal away, she screamed. Afterwards there was a dreadful silence.

Joan had not lost consciousness. Her healthy nerves stanchly received the anguish and the shock, nor did she make any further outcry. She pressed her forehead against the sharp edge of the shelf, she drove her nails into her hands, and at intervals she writhed from head to foot. Circles of pain spread from the deep burn on her shoulder, spread and shrank, to spread and shrink again. The bones of her shoulder and arm ached terribly; fire still seemed to be eating into her flesh. The air was full of the smell of scorched skin so that she tasted it herself. And hotter than her hurt her heart burned consuming its own tenderness and love and trust.

When this pain left her, when she was free of her bonds, no force nor fear would hold her to Pierre. She would leave him as she had left her father. She would go away. There was no place for her to go to, but what did that matter so long as she might escape from this horrible place and this infernal tormentor? She did not look about to see the actuality of Pierre's silence. She thought that he had dropped the brand and was sitting near the table with his face hidden. How long the stillness of pain and fury and horror lasted there was no one to reckon. It was most startlingly broken by a voice. "Who screamed for help?" it said, and at the same instant a draught of icy air smote Joan. The door had opened with suddenness and violence. With difficulty she mastered her pain and turned her head.

Pierre had staggered to his feet. Opposite him, framed against the open door filled with the wan whiteness of the snow, stood a spare, tall figure. The man wore his fur collar turned up about his chin and ears, his fur cap pulled down about his brow, a sharp aquiline nose stood out above frozen mustaches, keen and brilliant eyes searched the room. He carried his gun across his arm in readiness, and snuffed the air like a suspicious hound. Then he advanced a step toward Pierre.

"What devil's work have you been at?" said he, his voice cutting the ear in its sharpness of astonished rage, and his hand slid down along the handle of his gun.

Pierre, watching him like a lynx, side-stepped, crouched, whipped out his gun, and fired. At almost the same second the other's gun went off. Pierre dropped.

This time Joan's nerves gave way and the room, with its smell of scorched flesh, of powder, and of frost, went out from her horrified senses. For a moment the stranger's stern face and brilliant eyes made the approaching center of a great cloud of darkness, then it too went out.

CHAPTER VII

THE JUDGMENT OF GOD

THE man who had entered with such violence upon so violent a scene, stood waiting till the smoke of Pierre's discharge had cleared away, then, still holding his gun in readiness, he stepped across the room and bent over the fallen man.

"I've killed him!" he said, just above his breath, and added presently, "That was the judgment of God." He looked about, taking in every detail of the scene, the branding iron that had burnt its mark deep into the boards where Pierre had thrown it down, the glowing fire heaped high and blazing dangerously in the small room, the woman bound and burnt, the white night outside the uncurtained window.

Afterwards he went over to the woman, who drooped in her bonds with head hanging backward over the wounded shoulder. He untied the silk scarf and the rope and carried her, still unconscious, into the bedroom where he laid her on the bed and bathed her face in water. Joan's crown of hair had fallen about her neck and temples. Her bared throat and shoulder had the firm smoothness of marble, her lifeless face, its pure, full lips fallen apart, its long lids closed, black-fringed and black-browed, owing little of its beauty to color or expression, was at no loss in this deathlike composure and whiteness. The man dealt gently with her as though she had been a child. He found clean rags which he soaked in oil and placed over her burn, then he drew the coarse clothing about her and resumed his bathing of her forehead.

She gave a moaning sigh, her face contracted woefully, and she opened her eyes. The man looked into them as a curious child might look into an opened door.

"Did you see what happened?" he asked her when she had come fully to herself.

"Yes," Joan whispered, her lips shaking.

"I've killed the brute."

Her face became a classic mask of tragedy, the drawn brows, horrified eyes, and widened mouth.

"Pierre? Killed?" Her voice, hardly more than a whisper, filled the house with its agony.

"Are you sorry?" demanded her rescuer sternly. "Was he in the habit of tying you up or was this — branding — a special diversion?"

Joan turned her face away, writhed from head

"DID YOU SEE WHAT HAPPENED?"

to foot, put up her two hands between him and her agonizing memories.

The man rose and left her, going softly into the next room. There he stood in a tense attitude of thought, sat down presently with his long, narrow jaw in his hands and stared fixedly at Pierre. He was evidently trying to fight down the shock of the spectacle, grimly telling himself to become used to the fact that here lay the body of a man that he had killed. In a short time he seemed to be successful, his face grew calm. He looked away from Pierre and turned his mind to the woman.

"She can't stay here," he said presently, in the tone of a man who has fallen into the habit of talking aloud to himself. He looked about in a hesitant, doubtful fashion. "God!" he said abruptly and snapped his fingers and thumb. He looked angry. Again he bent over Pierre, examined him with thoroughness and science, his face becoming more and more calm. At the end he rose and with an air of authority he went in again to Joan. She lay with her face turned to the wall.

"It is impossible for you to stay here," said he in a voice of command. "You are not fit to take care of yourself, and I can't stay and take care of you. You must come with me. I think you can manage that. Your husband — if he is your husband — is dead. It may or may not be a matter for sorrow to you, but I should say that it ought not to be anything but a merciful release. Women are queer creatures, though. . . . However, whether you are in grief or in rejoicing, you can't stay here. By to-morrow or next day you'll need more nursing than you do now. I don't want to take you to a neighbor, even if there was one near enough, but I'll take you with me. Will you get ready now?"

His sure, even, commanding voice evidently had a hypnotizing effect upon the dazed girl. Slowly, wincing, she stood up, and with his help gathered together some of her belongings which he put in the pack he carried on his shoulders. She wrapped herself in her warmest outdoor clothing. He then put his hand upon her arm and drew her toward the door of that outer room. She followed him blindly with no will of her own, but, as he stopped to strap on his snowshoes, her face lightened with pain, and she made as if to run to Pierre's body. He stood before her, "Don't touch him," said he, and, turning himself, he glanced back at Pierre. In that glance he saw one of the lean, brown hands stir. His face became suddenly suffused, even his eyes grew shot with blood. Standing carefully so as to obstruct her view, he caught at the corner of an elk hide and threw it over Pierre. Then he went to Joan, who stared at him, white and shaking. He put his arm around her and drew her out, shutting the door of her home and leaning against it.

"You can't go back," said he gently and reasonably. "The man tried to kill you. You can't go back. Surely you meant to go away."

"Yes," said Joan, "yes. I did mean to go away. But — but it's Pierre."

He bent and began to strap on her snowshoes. There was a fighting brilliance in his eyes and a strange look of hurry about him that had its effect on Joan. "It's Pierre no longer," said he. "What can you do for him? What can he do for you? Be sensible, child. Come. Don't waste time. There will be snow to-day."

In fact it was to-day. The moon had set and a gray dawn possessed the world. It was not nearly so cold and the great range had vanished in a bank of gray-black clouds moving steadily northward under a damp wind. Joan looked at this one living creature with wide, fever-brightened eyes.

"Come," said the man impatiently.

Joan bent her head and followed him across the snow.

CHAPTER VIII

DELIRIUM

IT is not the people that have led still and uneventful lives who are best prepared for emergencies. They are not trained to face crises, to make prompt and just decisions. Joan had made but two such resolutions in her life; the first when she had followed Pierre, the second when she had kept Holliwell's books in defiance of her husband's jealousy. The leaving her father had been the result of long and painful thought. Now, in a few hours, events had crashed about her so that her whole life, outer and inner, had been shattered. Beyond the pain and fever of her wound there was an utter confusion of her faculties. Before she fainted she had, indeed, made a distinct resolve to leave Pierre. It was this purpose, working subconsciously on her will, as much as the urgent pressure of the stranger, that took her past Pierre's body out into the dawn and sent her on that rash journey of hers in the footsteps of an unknown man. This being seemed to her then hardly human. Mysteriously he had stepped in out of the night, mysteriously he had condemned Pierre, and in self-defense, for Joan had seen Pierre draw his gun and fire, he had killed her husband. Now, just as mysteriously, as inevitably it seemed to her, he took command of her life. She was a passive, shipwrecked thing — a derelict. She had little thought and no care for her life.

As the silent day slowly brightened through its glare of clouds, she plodded on, setting her snowshoes in the tracks her leader made. The pain in her shoulder steadily increased, more and more absorbed her consciousness. She saw little but the lean, resolute figure that went before her, turning back now and then with a look and a smile that were a compelling mixture of encouragement, pity, and command. She did not know that they were traveling north and west toward the wildest and most desolate country, that every time she set down her foot she set it down farther from humanity. She began soon to be a little light-headed and thought that she was following Pierre.

At noon they entered the woods, and her guide came beside her and led her through fallen timber and past pitfalls of soft snow. Suddenly, "I can't go no more," she sobbed, and stopped, swaying. At that he took her in his arms and carried her a few hundred feet till they entered a cabin under the shelter of firs.

"It's the ranger-station," said he; "the ranger told me that I could make use of it on my way back. We can pass the night here."

Joan knew that he had carried her across a strange room and put her on a strange bed. He took off her snowshoes, and she lay watching him light a fire in the cold, clean stove and cook a meal from supplies left by the owner of the house. She was trying now to remember who he was, what had happened, and why she was in such misery and pain. Sometimes she knew that he was her father and that she was at home in that wretched shack up Lone River, and an ineffable satisfaction would relax her cramped mind; sometimes, just as clearly, she knew that he was Pierre who had taken her away to some strange place, and, in this certainty, she was even more content. But always the horrible flame on her shoulder burnt her again to the confusion of half-consciousness. He was n't John Carver, he was n't Pierre. Who, in God's name, was he? And why was she here alone with him? She could not frame a question; she had a fear that, if she began to speak, she would scream and rave, would tell impossible, secret, sacred things. So she held herself to silence, to a savage watchfulness, to a battle with delirium.

The man brought her a cup of strong coffee and held up her head so that she could drink it, but it nauseated her and she thrust it weakly away, asking for cold water. After she had drunk this, her mind cleared for an instant and she tried to stand up.

"I must go back to Pierre now," she said, looking about with wild but resolute eyes.

"Lie still," said the stranger gently. "You're not fit to stir. Trust me. It's all right. You're quite safe. Get rested and well, then you may go wherever you like. I want only to help you."

The reassuring tone, the promising words coerced her and she dropped back. Presently, in spite of pain, she slept.

She woke and slept in fever for many hours, vaguely aware, at times, that she was traveling. She felt the motion of a sled under her and knew that she was lying on the warm hide of some freshly killed beast and that a blanket and a canvas covering protected her from a swirl of snow. Then she thought she heard a voice babbling queerly and saw a face quite terribly different from other human faces. The covering was taken from her, snowflakes touched her cheek, a lantern shone in her eyes, and she was lifted and carried into a warm, pleasant-smelling place from which were magically and completely banished all sound and bitterness of storm. She tried to see where she was, but her eyes looked on incredible colors and confusions, so she shut them and passively allowed herself to be handled by deft hands. She knew only that delicious coolness, cleanliness, and softness were given to her body, that the pain in her shoulder was soothed, that dreamlessly she slept.

CHAPTER IX

DRIED ROSE-LEAVES

THE house that Prosper Gael had built for himself and for the woman whom Joan came to think of as the "tall child," stood in a cañon, a deep, secret fold of the hills, where a cliff stood behind it, and where the pine-needled ground descended before its door, under the far-flung, greenish-brown shade of fir boughs, to the lip of a green lake. Here the highest snow-peak toppled giddily down and reared giddily up from the crystal green to the ether blue, firs massed into the center of the double image. In January, the lake was a glare of snow, in which the big firs stood deep, their branches heavily weighted. Prosper had dug a tunnel from his door through a big drift which touched his eaves. It was curious to see Wen Ho come pattering out of this Northern cave, his yellow, Oriental face and slant eyes peering past the stalactite icicles as though they felt their own incongruity almost with a sort of terror. The interior of the five-room house gave just such an effect of bizarre and extravagant contrast; an effect, too, of luxury, though in truth it was furnished for the most part with stuffs and objects picked up at no very great expense in San Francisco shops. Nevertheless, there was nothing tawdry and, here and there, something really precious. Draperies on the walls, furniture made by Wen Ho and Prosper, lacquered in black and red, brass and copper, bright pewter, gay china, some fur rugs, a gorgeous Oriental lamp, bookcases with volumes of a sober richness, in fact the costliest and most laborious of imports to this wilderness, small-paned, horizontal windows curtained in some heavy green-gold stuff which slipped along the black lacquered pole on rings of jade; all these and a hundred other points of softly brilliant color gave to the living-room a rare and striking look, while the bedrooms were matted, daintily furnished, carefully appointed as for a bride. Much thought and trouble, much detailed labor, had gone to the making of this odd nest in a Wyoming cañon. Whatever one must think of Prosper Gael, it is difficult to shirk heartache on his account. A man of his temperament does not lightly undertake even a companioned isolation in a winter land. To picture what place of torment this well-appointed cabin was to him before he brought to it Joan, as a lonely man brings in a wounded bird to nurse and cherish, stretches the fancy on a rack of varied painfulness.

On that night, snow was pouring itself down the narrow cañon in a crowded whirl of dry, clean flakes. Wen Ho, watchful, for his master was already a day or so beyond the promised date of his return, had started a fire on the hearth and spread a single cover on the table. He had drawn the green-and-gold curtains as though there had been anything but whirling whiteness to look in and stood warming himself with a rubbing of thin, dry hands before the open blaze. The real heat of the house, and it was almost unbearably hot, came from the stoves in kitchen and bedrooms, but this fire gave its quota of warmth and more than its quota of that beauty so necessary to Prosper Gael.

Wen Ho put his head from one side to the other and stopped rubbing his hands. He had heard the packing of snow under webs and runners. After listening a moment, he nodded to himself, like a figure in a pantomime, ran into the kitchen, did something to the stove, then lighted a lantern and pattered out along the tunnel dodging the icicle stalactites. Between the firs he stopped and held his lantern high so that it touched a moving radius of flakes to silver stars. Back of him through the open door streamed the glow of lamp and fire filling the icicles with blood and flushing the walls and the roof of the cave.

Down the cañon Prosper shouted, "Wen Ho! Wen Ho!"

The Chinaman plunged down the trail, packed below the new-fallen snow by frequent passage, and presently met the bent figure of his master pulling and breathing hard. Without speaking, Wen Ho laid hold of the sled rope and together the two men tugged up the last steep bit of the hill.

"Velly heavy load," said Wen.

Prosper's eyes, gleaming below the visor of his cap, smiled half-maliciously upon him. "It's a deer killed out of season," he said, "and other cattle — no maverick either — fairly marked by its owner. Lend me a hand and we'll unload."

Wen showed no astonishment. He removed the covering and peeped slantwise at the strange woman who stared at him unseeingly with large, bright eyes. She closed them, frowning faintly as though she protested against the intrusion of a Chinese face into her disturbed mental world.

The men took her up and carried her into the house, where they dressed her wound and laid her with all possible gentleness in one of the two beds of stripped and lacquered pine that stood in the bedroom facing the lake. Afterwards they moved the other bed and Prosper went in to his meal.

He was too tired to eat. Soon he pushed his plate away, turned his chair to face the fire, and, slipping down to the middle of his spine, stuck out his lean, long legs, locked his hands back of his head, let his chin fall, and stared into the flames.

Wen Ho removed the dishes, glancing often at his master.

"You velly tired?" he questioned softly.

"It was something of a pull in the storm."

"Velly small deer," babbled the Chinaman, "velly big lady."

Prosper smiled a queer smile that sucked in and down the corners of his mouth.

"She come after all?" asked Wen Ho.

Prosper's smile disappeared; he opened his eyes and turned a wicked, gleaming look upon his man. What with the white face and drawn mouth the look was rather terrible. Wen Ho vanished with an increase of speed and silence.

Alone, Prosper twisted himself in his chair till his head rested on his arms. It was no relaxation of weariness or grief, but an attitude of cramped pain. His face, too, was cramped when, a motionless hour later, he lifted it again. He got up then, broken with weariness, and went softly across the matted hall into the room where Joan slept, and he stood beside her bed.

A glow from the stove, and the light shining through the door, dimly illumined her. She was sleeping very quietly now; the flush of fever had left her face and it was clear of pain, quite simple and sad. Prosper looked at her and looked about the room as though he felt what he saw to be a dream. He put his hand on one long strand of Joan's black hair.

"Poor child!" he said. "Good child!" And went out softly, shutting the door.

In the bedroom where Joan came again to altered consciousness of life, there stood a blue china jar of potpourri, rose-leaves dried and spiced till they stored all the richness of a Southern summer. Joan's first question, strangely enough, was drawn from her by the persistence of this vague and pungent sweetness.

She was lying quietly with closed eyes, Prosper looking down at her, his finger on her even pulse, when, without opening her long lids, she asked, "What smells so good?"

Prosper started, drew away his fingers, then

answered, smiling, "It's a jar of dried rose-leaves. Wait a moment, I'll let you hold it."

He took the jar from the window sill and carried it to her.

She looked at it, took it in her hands, and when he removed the lid, she stirred the leaves curiously with her long forefinger.

"I never seen roses," she said, and added, "What's basil?"

Prosper was startled. For an instant all his suppositions as to Joan were disturbed. "Basil? Where did you ever hear of basil?"

"Isabella and Lorenzo," murmured Joan, and her eyes darkened with her memories.

Prosper found his heart beating faster than usual. "Who are you, you strange creature? I think it's time you told me your name. Have n't you any curiosity about me?"

"Yes," said Joan; "I've thought a great deal about you." She wrinkled her wide brows. "You must have been out after game, though 't was out of season. And you must have heard me a-cryin' out an' come in. That was right courageous, stranger. I would surely like you to know why I come away with you," she went on, wistful and weak, "but I don't know as how I can make it plain to you." She paused, turning the blue jar in her hand. "You're very strange to me," she said, "an' yet, someways, you takin' care of me so well an' so — so awful kind —" her voice gave forth its tremolo of feeling — "seems like I knowed you better than any other person in the world."

A flush came into his face.

"I would n't like you to be thinkin' —" She stopped, a little breathless.

He took the jar, sat down on the bed, and laid a hand firmly over both of hers. "I 'won't be thinking' anything," he said, "only what you would like me to think. Listen — when a man finds a wounded bird out in the winter woods, he'll bring it home to care for it. And he 'won't be thinking' the worse of its helplessness and tameness. Of course I know — but tell me your name, please!"

"Joan Landis."

At the name, given painfully, Joan drew a weighted breath, another, then, pushing herself up as though oppressed beyond endurance, she caught at Prosper's arm, clenched her fingers upon it, and bent her black head in a terrible paroxysm of grief. It was like a tempest. Prosper thought of storm-driven, rain-wet trees wild in a wind . . . of music, the prelude to "Fliegende

Holländer." Joan's weeping bent and rocked her. He put his arm about her, tried to soothe her. At her cry of "Pierre! Pierre!" he whitened, but suddenly she broke from him and threw herself back amongst the pillows.

"'T was you that killed him," she moaned. "What hev I to do with you?"

It was not the last time that bitter exclamation was to rise between them; more and more fiercely it came to wring his peace and hers. This time he bore it with a certain philosophy, calmed her patiently.

"How could I help it, Joan?" he pleaded. "You saw how it was?" As she grew quieter, he talked. "I heard you scream like a person being tortured to death — twice — a gruesome enough sound, let me tell you, to hear in the dead of a white, still night. I did n't altogether want to break into your house. I've heard some ugly stories about men venturing to disturb the work of murderers. But, you see, Joan, I've a fear of myself. I've a cruel brain. I can use it on my own failures. I've been through some self-punishment — no! of course, you don't understand all that. . . . Anyway, I came in, in great fear of my life, and saw what I saw — a woman tied up and devilishly tortured, a man gloating over her helplessness. Naturally, before I spoke my mind, as a man was bound to speak it, under the pain and fury of such a spectacle, I got ready to defend myself. Your — Pierre" — there was a biting contempt in his tone — "saw my gesture, whipped out his gun, and fired. My shot was half a second later than his. I might more readily have lost my life than taken his. If he *had* lived, Joan, could you have forgiven him?"

"No," sobbed Joan; "I think not." She trembled. "He said terrible hard words to me. He did n't love me like I loved him. He planned to put a brand on me so's I c'd be his own like as if I was a beast belongin' to him. Mr. Holliwell said right, I don't belong to no man. I belong to my own self."

The storm had passed into this troubled after-tossing of thought.

"Can you tell me about it all?" asked Prosper. "Would it help?"

"I could n't," she moaned; "no, I could n't Only — if I had n't 'a' left Pierre a-lyin' there alone. A dog that had onct loved him would n't 'a' done that." She sat up again, white and wild. "That's why I must go back. I must surely go. I must! Oh, I must!"

"Go back thirty miles through wet snow when

you can't walk across the room, Joan?" He smiled pityingly.

Her hands twisting in his, she stared past him, out through the window, where the still, sunny day shone blue through shadowy pine branches. Tears rolled down her face.

"Can't you go back?" She turned the desolate, haunted eyes upon him. "Oh, can't you? — to do some kindness to him? Can you ever stop a-thinkin' of him lyin' there?"

Prosper's face was hard through its gentleness. "I've seen too many dead men, less deserving of death. But, hush! — you lie down and go to sleep. I'll try to manage it. I'll try to get back and show him some kindness, as you say. There! Will you be a good girl now?"

She fell back and her eyes shone their gratitude upon him. "Oh, you are good!" she said. "When I'm well — I'll *work* for you!"

He shook his head, smiled, kissed her hand, and went out.

She was entirely exhausted by her emotion, so that all her memories fell away from her and left her in a peaceful blankness. She trusted Prosper's word. With every fiber of her heart she trusted him, as simply, as singly, as foolishly as a child trusts God.

CHAPTER X

PROSPER COMES TO A DECISION

PERHAPS, in spite of his gruesome boast as to dead men, it was as much to satisfy his own spirit as to comfort Joan's that Prosper actually did undertake a journey to the cabin that had belonged to Pierre. It was true that Prosper had never been able to stop thinking, not so much of the tall, slim youth lying so still across the floor, all his beauty and strength turned to an ashen slackness, as of a brown hand that stirred. The motion of those fingers groping for life had continually disturbed him. The man, to Prosper's mind, was an insensate brute, deserving of death, even of torment, most deserving of Joan's desertion, nevertheless, it was not easy to harden his nerves against the picture of a man left, wounded and helpless, to die slowly alone. Prosper went back expecting to find a dead man, went back as a murderer visits the scene of his crime. He dubbed himself more judge than murderer, but there was a restless misery of the imagination not to be quieted by names. He went back stealthily at dusk, choosing a dusk of wind-driven snow so that his tracks vanished as soon as made. It was very desolate — the blank surface of the world with its flying scud, the blank yellow-gray sky, the range, all iron and white, the blue-black scars of leafless trees, the green-black etchings of firs. The wind cut across like a scythe, sharp, but making no stir above the drift. It was all dead and dark — an underground world which, Prosper felt, never could have seen the sun, had no memory of sun nor moon nor stars. The roof of Pierre's cabin made a dark ridge above the snow, veiled in cloudy drift. He reached it with a cold heart and slid down to its window, cautiously bending his face near to the pane. He expected an interior already dark from the snow piled round the window, so he cupped his hands about his eyes. At once he let himself drop out of sight below the sill. There was a living presence in the house. Prosper had seen a bright fire, the smoke of which had been hidden by the snow-spray, a cot was drawn up before the fire, and a big, fair young man in tweeds whose face, rosy, sensitive, and quiet, was bent over the figure on the cot. A pair of large, white hands were carefully busy.

Prosper, crouched below the window, considered what he had seen. It was a week now since he had left Landis for a dying man. This big fellow in tweeds must have come soon after the shooting. Evidently he was not caring for a dead man. The black head on the pillow had moved. Now there came the sound of speech, just a bass murmur. This time the black head turned itself slightly and Prosper saw Pierre's face. He had seen it only twice before; once when it had looked up, fierce and crazed, at his first entrance into the house, once again when it lay with lifted chin and pale lips on the floor. But even after so scarce a memory, Prosper was startled by the change. Before, it had been the face of a man beside himself with drink and the lust of animal power and cruelty; now it was the wistful face of Pierre, drawn into a tragic mask like Joan's when she came to herself; a miserably haunted and harrowed face, hopeless as though it, too, like the outside world, had lost or had never had a memory of sun. Evidently he submitted to the dressing of his wound, but with a shamed and pitiful look. Prosper's whole impression of the man was changed, and with the change there began something like a struggle. He was afflicted by a crossing of purposes and a stumbling of intention.

He did not care to risk a second look. He crept away and fled into the windy dusk. He traveled with the wind like a blown rag, and, stopping only for a few hours' rest at the ranger station, made the journey home by morning of the second day. And on the journey he definitely made up his mind concerning Joan.

Prosper Gael was a man of deliberate, though passionate, imagination. He did not often act upon impulse, though his actions were often those attempted only by passion-driven or impulsive folk. Prosper could never plead thoughtlessness. He justified carefully his every action to himself. Those were cold, dark hours of deliberation as he let the wind drive him across the desolate land. When the wind dropped and a splendid, still dawn swept up into the clean sky, he was at peace with his own mind and climbed up the mountain trail with a half-smile on his face.

In the dawn, awake on her pillows, Joan was listening for him, and at the sound of his webs she sat up, pale to her lips. She did not know what she feared, but she was filled with dread. The restful stupor that had followed her storm of grief had spent itself and she was suffering again — waves of longing for Pierre, of hatred for him, alternately submerged her. All these bleak, gray hours of wind during which Wen Ho had pattered in and out with meals, with wood for her stove, with little questions as to her comfort, she had suffered as people suffer in a dream; a restless misery like the misery of the pine branches that leaped up and down before her window. The stillness of the dawn, with its sound of nearing steps, gave her a sickness of heart and brain, so that when Prosper came softly in at her door she saw him through a mist. He moved quickly to her side, knelt by her, took her hands. His touch at all times had a tingling charge of vitality and will.

"He has been cared for, Joan," said Prosper. "Some friend of his came and did all that was left to be done."

"Some friend?" In the pale, delicately expanding light Joan's face gleamed between its black coils of hair with eyes like enchanted tarns. In fact they had been haunted during his absence by images to shake her soul. Prosper could see in them reflections of those terrors that had been tormenting her. His touch pressed reassurance upon her, his eyes, his voice.

"My poor child! My dear! I'm glad I am back to take care of you! Cry. Let me comfort you. He has been cared for. He is not lying there alone. He is dead. Let's forgive him, Joan." He shook her hands a little, urgently, and a most painful memory of Pierre's beseeching grasp came upon Joan.

She wrenched away and fell back, quivering, but she did not cry, only asked in her most moving voice, "Who took care of Pierre — after I went away and left him dead?"

Prosper got to his feet and stood with his arms folded, looking wearily down at her. His mouth had fallen into rather cynical lines and there were puckers at the corners of his eyes. "Oh, a big, fair young man — a rosy boy-face, serious-looking, blue eyes."

Joan was startled and turned round. "It was Mr. Holliwell," she said, in a wondering tone. "Did you talk with him? Did you tell him —?"

"No. Hardly." Prosper shook his head. "I found out what he had done for your Pierre without asking unnecessary questions. I saw him, but he did not see me."

"He'll be comin' to get me," said Joan. It was an entirely unemotional statement of certainty.

Prosper pressed his lips into a line and narrowed his eyes upon her.

"Oh, he will?"

"Yes. He'll be takin' after me. He must 'a'

ben scairt by somethin' Pierre said in the town durin' their quarrel an' have come up after him to look out what Pierre would be doin' to me. . . . I wisht he'd 'a' come in time. . . . What must he be thinkin' of me now, to find Pierre a-lyin' there dead, an' me gone! He'll be takin' after me to bring me home."

Prosper would almost have questioned her then, his sharp face was certainly at that moment the face of an inquisitor, a set of keen and delicate instruments ready for probing, but so weary and childlike did she look, so weary and childlike was her speech, that he forbore. What did it matter, after all, what there was in her past? She had done what she had done, been what she had been. If the fellow had branded her for sin, why, she had suffered overmuch. Prosper admitted, that, unbranded as to skin, he was scarcely fit to put his dirty civilized soul under her clean and savage foot. Was the big, rosy chap her lover? She had spoken of a quarrel between him and Pierre? But her manner of speaking of him was scarcely in keeping with the thought, rather it was the manner of a child-soul relying on the Shepherd who would be "takin' after" some small, lost one. Well, he would have to be a superman to find her here with no trails to follow and no fingers to point. Pierre by now would have told his story — and Prosper knew instinctively that he would tell it straight; whatever madness the young savage might perpetrate under the influence of drink and jealousy, he would hardly, with that harrowed face, be apt at fabrications — they would be looking for Joan to come back, to go to the town, to some neighboring ranch. They would make a search, but winter would be against them with its teeth bared, a blizzard was on its way. By the time they found her, thought Prosper, — and he quoted one of Joan's quaint phrases to himself, smiling with radiance as he did so, — "she won't be carin' to leave me." In his gay, little, firelit room, he sat, stretched out, lank and long, in the low, deep, red-lacquered chair, dozing through the long day, sipping strong coffee, smoking, reading. He was singularly quiet and content. The devil of disappointment and of thwarted desire that had wived him in this carefully appointed hiding-place stood away a little from him and that wizard imagination of his began to weave. By dusk, he was writing furiously and there was a glow of rapture on his face.

CHAPTER XI

THE WHOLE DUTY OF WOMAN

JOAN waited for Holliwell and, waiting, began inevitably to regain her strength. One evening as Wen Ho was spreading the table, Prosper looked up from his writing to see a tall, gaunt girl clinging to the door-jamb. She was dressed in the heavy clothes, which hung loose upon her long bones, her throat was drawn up to support the sharpened and hollowed face in which her eyes had grown very large and wistful. Her hair was braided and wrapped across her brow, her long, strong hands, smooth and only faintly brown, were thin, too, and curiously expressive as they clung to the logs. She was a moving figure, piteous, lovely, rather like some graceful mountain beast, its spirit half-broken by wounds and imprisonment and human tending, but ready to leap into a savagery of flight or of attack. They were wild, those great eyes, as well as wistful. Prosper, looking suddenly up at them, caught his breath. He put down his book as quietly as though she had indeed been a wild, easily startled thing, and, suppressing the impulse to rise, stayed where he was, leaning a trifle forward, his hands on the arms of his chair.

Joan's eyes wandered curiously about the brilliant room and came to him at last. Prosper met them, relaxed, and smiled.

"Come in and dine with me, Joan," he said. "Tell me how you like it."

She felt her way weakly to the second large chair and sat down facing him across the hearth. The Chinaman's shadow, thrown strongly by the lamp, ran to and fro between and across them. It was a strange scene truly, and Prosper felt with exhilaration all its strangeness. This was no Darby and Joan fireside; a wizard with his enchanted leopardess, rather. He was half-afraid of Joan and of himself.

"It's right beautiful," said Joan, "an' right strange to me. I never seen anything like it before. That" — her eyes followed Wen Ho's departure half-fearfully — "that man and all."

Prosper laughed delightedly, stretching up his arms in full enjoyment of her splendid ignorance. "The Chinaman? Does he look so strange to you?"

"Is that what he is? I — I did n't know." She smiled rather sadly and ashamedly. "I'm awful ignorant, Mr. Gael. I just can read an' I've only read two books." She flushed and her pupils grew large.

Prosper saw that this matter of reading trod closely on her pain.

"Yes, he's a Chinaman from San Francisco. You know where that is."

"Yes, sir. I've heard talk of it — out on the Pacific Coast, a big city."

"Full of bad yellow men and a few good ones of whom let's hope Wen Ho is one. And full of bric-à-brac like all these things that surprise you so. Do you like bright colors, Joan?"

She pondered in the unself-conscious and unhurried fashion of the West, stroking the yellow, spotted skin that lay over the black arm of her chair and letting her eyes flit like butterflies in a garden on a zigzag journey to one after another of the flowers of color in the room.

"Well, sir," she said, "I c'd take to 'em better if they was more one at a time. I mean" — she pushed up the braid a little from wrinkling brows — "jest blue is awful pretty an' jest green. They're sort of cool, an' yeller, that's sure fine. You'd like to take it in your hands. Red is most too much like feelin' things. I dunno, it most hurts an' yet it warms you up, too. If I hed to live here —"

Prosper's eyebrows lifted a trifle.

"I'd — sure clear out the whole of this" — and she swept a ruthless hand.

Again Prosper made delighted use of that upward stretching of his arms. He laughed. "And you'd clear me out, too, would n't you? — if you *had* to live here."

"Oh, no," said Joan. She paused and fastened her enormous, grave look upon him. "I'd like right soon now to begin to work for you."

Again Prosper laughed. "Why," said he, "you don't know the first thing about woman's work, Joan. What could you do?"

Joan straightened wrathfully. "I sure do know. Sure I do. I can cook fine. I can make a room clean. I can launder —"

"Oh, pooh! The Chinaman does all that as well — no, better than you ever could do it. That's not woman's work."

Joan saw all the business of femininity swept off the earth. Profound astonishment, incredulity, and alarm possessed her mind and so her face. Truly, thought Prosper, it was like talking to a grave, trustful, and most impressionable child, the way she sat there, rather on the edge of her chair, her hands folded, letting everything he said disturb and astonish the whole pool of her thought.

"But, Mr. Gael, sweepin', washin', cookin', — ain't all that a woman's work?"

"Men can do it so much better," said Prosper, blowing forth a cloud of blue cigarette smoke and brushing it impatiently aside so that he could smile at her evident offense and perplexity.

"But they don't do it better. They're as messy an' uncomfortable as they can be when there ain't no woman to look after 'em."

"Not if they get good pay for keeping themselves and other people tidy. Look at Wen Ho."

"Oh," said Joan, "that ain't properly a man."

Prosper laughed out again. It was good to be able to laugh.

"I've known plenty of real white men who could cook and wash better than any woman."

"But — but what is a woman's work?"

Prosper remained thoughtful for a while, his head thrown back a little, looking at her through his eyelashes. In this position he was extraordinarily striking. His thin, sharp face gained by the slight foreshortening and his brilliant eyes, keen nose, and high brow did not quite so completely overbalance the sad and delicate strength of mouth and chin. In Joan's eyes, used to the obvious, clear beauty of Pierre, Gael was an ugly fellow, but even she, artistically untrained, caught at the moment the picturesqueness and grace of him, the mysterious lines of texture, of race; the bold chiselings of thought and experience. The colors of the room became him, too, for he was dark, with curious, catlike, greenish eyes.

"The whole duty of woman, Joan," he said, opening these eyes upon her, "can be expressed in just one little word — *charm.*"

And again at her look of mystification he laughed aloud.

"There's — there's babies," suggested Joan after a pause during which she evidently wrestled in vain with the true meaning of his speech.

"Dinner is served," said Prosper, rising quickly, and, getting back of her, he pushed her chair to the table, hiding in this way a silent paroxysm of mirth.

At dinner, Prosper, unlike Holliwell, made no attempt to draw Joan into talk, but sipped his wine and watched her, enjoying her composed silence and her slow, graceful movements. Afterwards he made a couch for her on the floor before the fire, two skins and a golden cushion, a rug of dull blue which he threw over her, hiding the ugly skirt and boots. He took a violin from the wall and tuned it, Joan watching him with all her eyes.

"I don't like what you're playin' now," she told him, impersonally and gently.

"I'm tuning up."

"Well, sir, I'd be gettin' tired of that if I was you."

"I'm almost done," said Prosper humbly.

He stood up near her feet at the corner of the hearth, tucked the instrument under his chin and played. It was the "Aubade Provençale," and he played it creditably, with fair skill and with some of the wizardry that his nervous vitality gave to everything he did. At the first note Joan started, her pupils enlarged, she lay still. At the end he saw that she was quivering and in tears.

He knelt down beside her, drew the hands from her face. "Why, Joan, what's the matter? Don't you like music?"

Joan drew a shaken breath. "It's as if it shook me in here, something trembles in my heart," she said. "I never heerd music before, jest whistlin'." And again she wept.

Prosper stayed there on his knee beside her, his chin in his hand. What an extraordinary being this was, what a magnificent wilderness. The thought of exploration, of discovery, of cultivation, filled him with excitement and delight. Such opportunities are rarely given to a man.

Even that other most beautiful adventure — yes, he could think this already! — might have been tame beside this one. He looked long at Joan, long into the fire, and she lay still, with the brooding beauty of that first-heard melody upon her face.

It was the first music she had ever heard, "except whistlin'," but there had been a great deal of "whistlin'" about the cabin up Lone River; whistling of robins in spring — nothing sweeter — the chordlike whistlings of thrush and vireo after sunset, that bubbling "mar-guer-ite" with which the blackbirds woo, and the light *diminuendo* with which the bluebird caressed the air after an April flight. Perhaps Joan's musical faculty was less untrained than any other. After all, that "Aubade Provençale" was just the melodious story of the woods in spring. Every note linked itself to an emotional, subconscious memory. It filled Joan's heart with the freshness of childhood and pained her only because it struck a spear of delight into her pain. She was eighteen, she had grown like a tree, drinking in sunshine and storm, but rooted to a solitude where very little else but sense-experience could reach her mind. She had seen tragedies of animal life, lonely death-struggles, horrible flights and more horrible captures, she had seen joyous wooings, love-pinings, partings, and bereavements. She had seen maternal fickleness and maternal constancy, maternal savagery; the end of mated bliss and its — renewal. She had seen the relentless catastrophes of storm. There had been starving winters and renewing springs, sad beautiful autumns, the riotous waste and wantonness of summer. These had all been objective experiences, but Joan's untamed and undistracted heart had taken them in deeply and deeply pondered upon them. There was no morality in their teachings, unless it was the morality of complete suspension of any judgment whatsoever, the marvelous literal, "Judge not." She knew that the sun shone on the evil and on the good, but she knew also that frost fell upon the good as well as upon the evil nor was the evil to be readily distinguished. Her father prated of only one offense, her mother's sin. Joan knew that it was a man's right to kill his woman for "dealin's with another man." This law was human; it evidently did not hold good with animals. There was no bitterness, though some ferocity, in the traffic of their loves.

While she pondered through the first sleepless nights in this strange shelter of hers, and while the blizzard Prosper had counted on drove bayoneted battalions of snow across the plains and forced them, screaming like madmen, along the narrow cañon, Joan came slowly and fully to a realization of the motive of Pierre's deed. He had been jealous. He had thought that she was having dealings with another man. She grew hot and shamed. It was her father's sin, that branding on her shoulder, or, perhaps, going back farther, her mother's sin. Carver had warned Pierre — of the hot and smothered heart — to beware of Joan's "lookin' an' lookin' at another man." Now, in piteous woman fashion, Joan went over and over her memories of Pierre's love, altering them to fit her terrible experience. It was a different process from that simple seeing of pictures in the fire from which she had been startled by Pierre's return. A man's mind in her situation would have been intensely occupied with thoughts of the new companion, but Joan, thorough as a woman always is, had not yet caught up. She was still held by all the strong mesh of her short married life. She had simply not got as far as Prosper Gael. She accepted his hospitality vaguely, himself even more vaguely. When she would be done with her passionate grief, her laborious going-over of the past, her active and tormenting anger with the lover whom Prosper had told her was dead, then it would be time to study this other man. As for her future, she had no plans at all. Joan's life came to her as it comes to a child, unsullied by curiosity. At this time Prosper was infinitely the more curious, the more excited of the two.

CHAPTER XII

A MATTER OF TASTE

"WHAT are you writin' so hard for, Mr. Gael?" Joan voiced the question wistfully on the height of a long breath. She drew it from a silence which seemed to her to have filled this strange, gay house for an eternity. For the first time full awareness of the present cut a rift in the troubled cloudiness of her introspection. She had been sitting in her chair, listless and wan, now staring at the flames, now following Wen Ho's activities with absent eyes. A storm was swirling outside. Near the window, Prosper, a figure of keen absorption, bent over his writing-table, his long, fine hand driving the pencil across sheet after sheet. He looked like a machine, so regular and rapid was his work. A sudden sense of isolation came upon Joan. What part had she in the life of this companion, this keeper of her own life? She felt a great need of drawing nearer to him, of finding the humanity in him. At first she fought the impulse, reserve, pride, shyness locking her down, till at last her nerves gave her such torment that her fingers knitted into each other and on the outbreathing of a desperate sigh she spoke.

"What are you writin' so hard for, Mr. Gael?"

At once Prosper's hand laid down its pencil and he turned about in his chair and gave her a gleaming look and smile. Joan was fairly startled. It was as if she had touched some mysterious spring and turned on a dazzling, unexpected light. As a matter of fact, Prosper's heart had leapt at her wistful and beseeching voice.

He had been biding his time. He had absorbed himself in writing, content to leave in suspense the training of his enchanted leopardess. Half-absent glimpses of her desolate beauty as she moved about his winter-bound house, contemplation of her unself-consciousness as she companioned his meals, the pleasure he felt in her rapt listening to his music in the still, frost-held evenings by the fire — these he had made enough. They quieted his restlessness, soothed the ache of his heart, filled him with a warm and patient desire, different from any feeling he had yet experienced. He was amused by her lack of interest in him. He was not accustomed to such *through-gazing* from beautiful eyes, such incurious absence of questioning. She evidently accepted him as a superior being, a Providence; he was not a man at all, not of the same clay as Pierre and herself. Prosper had waited understandingly enough for her first move. When the personal question came, it made a sort of crash in the expectant silence of his heart.

Before answering, except by that smile, he lit himself a cigarette; then, strolling to the fire, he sat on the rug below her, drawing his knees up into his hands.

"I'd like to tell you about my writing, Joan. After all, it's the great interest of my life, and I've been fairly seething with it; only I did n't want to bother you, worry your poor, distracted head."

"I never thought," said Joan slowly, "I never thought you'd be carin' to tell me things. I know so awful little."

"It was n't your modesty, Joan. It was simply because you have n't given me a thought since I dragged you in here on my sled. I've been nothing" — under the careless, half-bitter manner, he was weighing his words and their probable effect — "nothing, for all these weeks, but — a provider."

"A provider?" Joan groped for the meaning of the word. It came, and she flushed deeply. "You mean I've just taken things, taken your kind doin's toward me an' not been givin' you a thought." Her eyes filled and shone mortification down upon him so that he put his hand quickly over hers, tightened together on her knee.

"Poor girl! I'm not reproaching you."

"But, Mr. Gael, I wanted to work for you. You would n't let me." She brushed away her tears. "What can I do? Where can I go?"

"You can stay here and make me happy as you have been doing ever since you came. I was very unhappy before. And you can give me just as much or as little attention as you please. I don't ask you for a bit more. Suppose you stop grieving, Joan, and try to be just a little happier yourself. Take an interest in life. Why, you poor, young, ignorant child, I could open whole worlds of excitement, pleasure, to you, if you'd let me. There's more in life than you've dreamed of experiencing. There's music, for one thing, and there are books and beauty of a thousand kinds, and big, wonderful thoughts, and there's companionship and talk. What larks we could have, you and I, if you would care — I mean, if you would wake up and let me show you how. You do want to learn a woman's work, don't you, Joan?"

She shook her head slowly, smiling wistfully, the tears gone from her eyes, which were puzzled, but diverted from pain. "I did n't savvy what you meant when you talked about what a woman's work rightly was. An' I'm so awful ignorant, you know so awful much. It scares me, plumb scares me, to think how much you know, more than Mr. Holliwell! Such books an' books an' books! An' writin' too. You see I'd be no help nor company fer you. I'd like to listen to you. I'd listen all day long, but I'd not be understandin'. No more than I understand about that there woman's work idea."

He laughed at her, keeping reassuring eyes on hers. "I can explain anything. I can make you understand anything. I'll grant you, my idea of a woman's work is difficult for you to get hold of. That's a big question, after all, one of the biggest. But — just to begin with and we'll drop it later for easier things — I believe, the world believes, that a woman ought to be beautiful. You can understand that?"

Joan shook her head. "It's a awful hard sayin', Mr. Gael. It's awful hard to say you had ought to be somethin' a person can't manage for themselves. I mean —" poor Joan, the inarticulate, floundered, but he left her, rather cruelly, to flounder out. "I mean, that's an awful hard sayin' fer a homely woman, Mr. Gael."

He laughed. "Oh," said he with a gesture, "there is no such thing as a homely woman. A homely woman simply does not count." He got up, looked for a book, found it, opened it, and brought it to her. "Look at that picture, Joan. What do you think of it?"

It was of a woman, a long-drawn, emaciated creature, extraordinarily artificial in her grace and in the pose and expression of her ugly, charming form and features. She had been aided by hair-dresser and costumer and by her own wit, aided into something that made of her an arresting and compelling picture. "What do you think of her, Joan?" smiled Prosper Gael.

Joan screwed up her eyes distastefully. "Ain't she queer, Mr. Gael? Poor thing, *she's* homely!"

He clapped to the book. "A matter of educated taste," he said. "You don't know beauty when you see it. If you walked into a drawing-room by the side of that marvelous being, do you think you'd win a look, my dear girl? Why, your great brows and your great, wild eyes and your face and form of an Olympian and your free grace of a forest beast — why, they would n't be noticed. Because, Joan, that queer, poor thing knew woman's work from A to Z. She's beautiful, Joan, beautiful as God most certainly never intended her to be. Why, it's a triumph — it's something to blow a trumpet over. It's art!"

He returned the volume and came back to stand by the mantel, half-turned from her, looking down into the fire. For the moment, he had created in himself a reaction against his present extraordinary experiment, his wilderness adventure. He was keenly conscious of a desire for civilized woman, for her practiced tongue, her poise, her matchless companionship. . . .

Joan spoke, "You mean I'm awful homely, Mr. Gael?"

The question set him to laughing outrageously. Joan's pride was stung.

"You've no right to laugh at me," she said. "I'd not be carin' what you think." And she left him, moving like an angry stag, head high, light-stepping.

He went back to his work, not at all in regret at her pique and still amused by the utter femininity of her simple question.

Before dinner he rapped at her door. "Joan, will you do me a favor?"

A pause, then, in her sweet, vibrant voice, she

answered, "I'd be doin' anything fer you, Mr. Gael."

"Then, put on these things for dinner instead of your own clothes, will you?"

She opened the door and he piled into her arms a mass of shining silk, on top of it a pair of gorgeous Chinese slippers.

"Do it to please me, even if you think it makes you look queer, will you, Joan?"

"Of course," she smiled, looking up from the gleaming, sliding stuff into his face. "I'd like to, anyway. Dressing-up — that's fun."

And she shut the door.

She spread the silk out on the bed and found it a loose robe of dull blue, embroidered in silver dragons and lined with brilliant rose. There was a skirt of this same rose-colored stuff. In one weighted pocket she found a belt of silver coins and a little vest of creamy lace. There were rose silk stockings stuffed into the shoes. Joan eagerly arrayed herself. She had trouble with the vest, it was so filmy, so vaguely made, it seemed to her, and to wear it at all she had to divest herself altogether of the upper part of her coarse underwear. Then it seemed to her startlingly inadequate even as an undergarment. However, the robe did go over it, and she drew that close and belted it in. It was provided with long sleeves and fell to her ankles. She thrilled at the delightful clinging softness of silk stockings and for the first time admired her long, round ankles and shapely feet. The Chinese slippers amused her, but they too were beautiful, all embroidered with flowers and dragons.

She felt she must look very queer, indeed, and went to the mirror. What she saw there surprised her because it was so strange, so different. Pierre had not dealt in compliments. His woman was his woman and he loved her body. To praise this body, surrendered in love to him, would have been impossible to the reverence and reserve of his passion.

Now, Joan brushed and coiled her hair, arranging it instinctively, but perhaps a little in imitation of that queer picture that had looked to her so hideous. Then, starting toward the door at Wen Ho's announcement of "Dinner, lady," she was quite suddenly overwhelmed by shyness. From head to foot for the first time in all her life she was acutely conscious of herself.

CHAPTER XIII

THE TRAINING OF A LEOPARDESS

ON that evening Prosper began to talk. The unnatural self-repression he had practiced gave way before the flood of his sociability. It was Joan's amazing beauty as she stumbled wretchedly into the circle of his firelight, her neck drawn up to its full length, her head crowned high with soft, black masses, her lids dropped under the weight of shyness, vivid fright in her distended pupils, scarlet in her cheeks, — Joan's beauty of long, strong lines draped to advantage for the first time in soft and clinging fabrics,— that touched the spring of Prosper's delighted egotism. There it was again, the ideal audience, the necessary atmosphere, the beautiful, gracious, intelligent listener. He forgot her ignorance, her utter simplicity, the unplumbed emptiness of her experience, and he spread out his colorful thoughts before her in colorful words, the mental plumage of civilized courtship.

After dinner, now sipping from the small coffee cup in his hand, now setting it down to move excitedly about the room, he talked of his life, his book, his plans. He told anecdotes, strange adventures; he drew his own inverted morals; he sketched his fantastic opinions; he was in truth fascinating, a speaking face, a lithe, brilliant presence, a voice of edged persuasion. He turned witty phrases. Poor Joan! One sentence in ten she understood and answered with her slow smile and her quaint, murmured, "Well!" His eloquence did her at least the service of making her forget herself. She was rather crestfallen because he had not complimented her; his veiled look of appreciation, this coming to of his real self was too subtle a flattery for her perception. Nevertheless, his talk pleased her. She did not want to disappoint him, so she drew herself up straight in the big red-lacquered chair, sipped her coffee in dainty imitation of him, gave him the full, deep tribute of her gaze, asked for no explanations and let the astounding statements he made, the amazing pictures he drew, cut their way indelibly into her most sensitive and preserving memory.

Afterwards, at night, for the first time she did not weep for Pierre, the old lost Pierre who had so changed into a torturer, but, wakeful, her brain on fire, she pondered over and over the things she had just heard, feeling after their meaning, laying aside for future enlightenment what was utterly incomprehensible, arguing with herself as to the truth of half-comprehended speeches — an ignorant child wrestling with a modern philosophy, tricked out in motley by a ready wit.

There were more personal memories that gave her a flush of pleasure, for after midnight, as she was leaving him, he came near to her, took her hand with a grateful "Joan, you've done so much for me to-night, you've made me happy," and the request, "You won't put your hair back to the old way, will you? You will wear pretty things, if I give them to you, won't you?" in a beseeching spoiled-boy's voice, very amusing and endearing to her.

He gave her the "pretty things," whole quantities of them, fine linen to be made up into underwear, soft white and colored silks and crêpes, which Joan, remembering the few lessons in dressmaking she had had from Maud Upper and with some advice from Prosper, made up not too awkwardly, accepting the mystery of them as one of Prosper's magic-makings. And, in the meantime, her education went on. Prosper read aloud to her, gave her books to read to herself, questioned her, tutored her, scolded her so fiercely sometimes that Joan would mount scarlet cheeks and open angry eyes. One day she fairly flung her book from her and ran out of the room, stamping her feet and shedding tears. But back she came presently for more, thirsting for knowledge, eager to meet her trainer on more equal grounds, to be able to answer him to some purpose, to contradict him, to stagger ever so slightly the self-assurance of his superiority.

And Prosper enjoyed the training of his captive leopardess, though he sometimes all but melted over the pathos of her and had much ado to keep his hands from her unconscious young beauty.

"You're so changed, Joan," he said one day abruptly. "You've grown as thin as a reed, child; I can see every bone, and your eyes — don't you ever shut them any more?"

Joan, prone on the skin before the fire, elbows on the fur, hands to her temples, face bent over a book, looked up impatiently.

"I'd not be talkin' now if I was you, Mr. Gael. You had ought to be writin' an' I 'm readin'. I can't talk an' read; seems when I do a thing I just hed to *do* it!"

Prosper laughed and returned chidden to his task, but he could n't help watching her, lying there in her blue frock across his floor, like a tall, thin Magdalene, all her rich hair fallen wildly about her face. She was such a child, such a child!

CHAPTER XIV

JOAN RUNS AWAY

IT was a January night when Joan, her rough head almost in the ashes, had read "Isabella and the Pot of Basil" by the light of flames. It was in March, a gray, still afternoon, when, looking through Prosper's bookcase, she came upon the tale again.

Prosper was outdoors cutting a tunnel, freshly blocked with snow, and Joan, having finished the "Life of Cellini," a writer she loathed, but whose gorgeous fabrications her master had forced her to read, now hurried to the book-shelves in search of something more to her taste. She had the gay air of a holiday-seeker, returned "Cellini" with a smart push, and kneeling, ran her finger along the volumes, pausing on a binding of bright blue-and-gold. It was the color that had pleased her and the fat, square shape, also the look of fair and well-spaced type. She took the book and squatted on the rug happy as a child with a new toy of his own choosing.

And then she opened her volume in its middle and her eye looked upon familiar lines —

"So the two brothers and their murdered man —"

Joan's heart fell like a leaden weight and the color dropped from her face. In an instant she was back in Pierre's room and the white night circled her in great silence and she was going over the story of her love and Pierre's — their love, their beautiful, grave, simple love that had so filled her life. And now where was she? In the house of the man who had killed her husband! She had been waiting for Holliwell, but for a long while now she had forgotten that. Why was she still here? A strange, guilty terror came with the question. She looked down at the soft, yellow crêpe of the dress she had just made and she looked at her hands lying white and fine and useless, and she felt for the high comb Prosper had put into her hair. Then she stared around the gorgeous little room, snug from the world, so secret in its winter cañon. She heard Wen Ho's incessant pattering in the kitchen, the crunch and thud of Prosper's shoveling outside. It was suddenly a horrible nightmare, or less a nightmare than a dream, pleasant in the dreaming, but hideous to an awakened mind. She was awake. Isabella's story had thrown her mind, so abruptly dislocated, back to a time before the change, back to her old normal condition of a young wife. That little homestead of Pierre's! Such a hunger opened in her soul that she bent her head and moaned. She could think of nothing now but those two familiar, bare, clean rooms — Pierre's gun, Pierre's rod, her own coat there by the door, the snowshoes. There was no place in her mind for the later tragedy. She had gone back of it. She would rather be alone in her own home, desolate though it was, than anywhere else in all the homeless world.

And what could prevent her from going? She laughed aloud, — a short, defiant laugh, — rippled to her feet, and, in her room, took off Prosper's "pretty things" and got into her own old clothes; the coarse underwear, the heavy stockings and boots, the rough skirt, the man's shirt. How loosely they all hung! How thin she was! Now into her coat, her woolen cap down over her ears, her gloves — she was ready, her heart laboring like an exhausted stag's, her knees trembling, her wrists mysteriously absent. She went into the hall, found her snowshoes, bent to tie them on, and, straightening up, met Prosper who had come in out of the snow.

He was glowing from exercise, but at sight of her and her pale excitement, the glow left him and his face went bleak and grim. He put out his hand and caught her by the arm and she backed from him against the wall — this before either of them spoke.

"Where are you going, Joan?"

"I'm a-goin' home."

He let go of her arm. "You were going like this, without a word to me?"

"Mr. Gael," she panted, "I had a feelin' like you would n't 'a' let me go."

He turned, threw open the door, and stepped aside. She confronted his white anger.

"Mr. Gael, I left Pierre dead. I've been a-waitin' for Mr. Holliwell to come. I'm strong now. I must be a-goin' home." Suddenly, she blazed out: "You killed my man. What hev I to do with you?"

He bowed. Her breast labored and all the distress of her soul, troubled by an instinctive, inarticulate consciousness of evil, wavered in her eyes. Her reason already accused her of ingratitude and treachery, but every fiber of her had suddenly revolted. She was all for liberty, she must have it.

He was wise, made no attempt to hold her, let her go; but, as she fled under the firs, her webs sinking deep into the heavy, uncrusted snow, he stood and watched her keenly. He had not failed to notice the trembling of her body, the quick lift and fall of her breast, the rapid flushing and paling of her face. He let her go.

And Joan ran, drawing recklessly on the depleted store of what had always been her inexhaustible strength. The snow was deep and soft, heavy with moisture, the March air was moist, too, not keen with frost, and the green firs were softly dark against an even, stone-colored sky of cloud. To Joan's eyes, so long imprisoned, it was all astonishingly beautiful, clean and grave, part of the old life back to which she was running. Down the cañon trail she floundered, her short skirt gathering a weight of snow, her webs lifting a mass of it at every tugging step. Her speed perforce slackened, but she plodded on, out of breath and in a sweat. She was surprised at the weakness; put it down to excitement. "I was afeered he'd make me stay," she said, and, "I've got to go. I've got to go." This went with her like a beating rhythm. She came to the opening in the firs, the foot of the steep trail, and out there stretched the valley, blank snow, blank sky, here and there a wooded ridge, then a range of lower hills, blue, snow-mottled; not a roof, not a thread of smoke, not a sound.

"I'm awful far away," Joan whispered to herself, and, for the first time in her life, she doubted her strength. "I don't rightly know where I am." She looked back. There stood a high, familiar peak, but so were the outlines of these mountains jumbled and changed that she could not tell if Prosper's cañon lay north or south of Pierre's homestead. The former was high up on the foothills, and Pierre's was well down, above the river. From where she stood, there was no river-bed in sight. She tried to remember the journey, but nothing came to her except a confused impression of following, following, following. Had they gone toward the river first and then turned north or had they traveled close to the base of the giant range? The ranger's cabin where they had spent the night, surely that ought to be visible. If she went farther out, say beyond the wooded spur which shut the mountain country from her sight, perhaps she would find it. . . . She braced her quivering muscles and went on. The end of the jutting foothills seemed to crawl forward with her. She plunged into drifts, struggled up; sometimes the snow-plane seemed to stand up like a wall in front of her, the far hills lolling like a dragon along its top. She could not keep the breath in her lungs. Often she sank down and rested; when things grew steady she got up and worked on. Each time she rested, she crouched longer; each time made slower progress; and always the goal she had set herself, the end of that jutting hill, thrust itself out, nosed forward, sliding down to the plain. It began to darken, but Joan thought that her sight was failing. The enormous efforts she was making took every atom of her will. At last her muscles refused obedience, her laboring heart stopped. She stood a moment, swayed, fell, and this time she made no effort to rise. She had become a dark spot on the snow, a lifeless part of the loneliness and silence.

Above her, where the sharp peaks touched the clouds, there came a widening rift showing a cold, turquoise clarity. The sun was just setting and, as the cloud-banks lifted, strong shadows, intensely blue, pointed across the plain of snow. A small, black, energetic figure came out from among the firs and ran forward where the longest shadow pointed. It looked absurdly tiny and anxious; futile, in its pigmy haste, across the exquisite stillness. Joan, lying so still, was acquiescent; this little striving thing rebelled. It came forward steadily, following Joan's uneven tracks, stamping them down firmly to make a solid path, and, as the sun dropped, leaving an immense gleaming depth of sky, he came down and bent over the black speck that was Joan. . . .

Prosper took her by the shoulder and turned her over a little in the snow. Joan opened her eyes and looked at him. It was the dumb look of a beaten dog.

"Get up, child," he said, "and come home with me."

She struggled to her feet, he helping her; and silently, just as a savage woman, no matter what her pain, will follow her man, so Joan followed the track he had made by pressing the snow down triply over her former steps. "Can you do it?" he asked once, and she nodded. She was pale, her eyes heavy, but she was glad to be found, glad to be saved. He saw that, and he saw a dawning confusion in her eyes. At the end he drew her arm into his, and, when they came into the house, he knelt and took the snowshoes from her feet, she drooping against the wall. He put a hand on each of her shoulders and looked reproach.

"You wanted to leave me, Joan? You wanted to leave me, as much as that?"

She shook her head from side to side, then, drawing away, she stumbled past him into the room, dropped to the bearskin rug, and held out her hands to the flames. "It's awful good to be

JOAN, LYING SO STILL, WAS ACQUIESCENT

back," she said, and fell to sobbing. "I did n't think you'd be carin' — I was thinkin' only of old things. I was homesick — me that has no home."

Her shaken voice was so wonderful a music that he stood listening with sudden tears in his eyes.

"An' I can't ferget Pierre nor the old life, Mr. Gael, an' when I think 't was you that killed him, why, it breaks my heart. Oh, I know you hed to do it. I saw. An' I know I could n't 'a' stayed with him no more. What he did, it made me hate him — but you can't be thinkin' how it was with Pierre an' me before that night. We — we was happy. I ust to live with my father, Mr. Gael, an' he was an awful man, an' there was no lovin' between us, but when I first seen Pierre lookin' up at me, I first knowed what lovin' might be like. I just came away with him because he asked me. He put his hand on my arm an' said, 'Will you be comin' home with me, Joan Carver?' That was the way of it. Somethin' inside of me said, 'Yes,' fer all I was too scairt to do anything but look at him an' shake my head. An' the next mornin' he was there with his horses. Oh, Mr. Gael, I can't ferget him, even for hatin'. That brand on my shoulder, it's all healed, but my heart's so hurted, it's so hurted. An' when I come to thinkin' of how kind an' comfortin' you are an' what you've been a-doin' fer me, why, then, at the same time, I can't help but thinkin' that you killed my Pierre. You killed him. Fergive me, please; I would love you if I could, but somethin' makes me shake away from you — because Pierre's dead."

Again she wept, exhausted, broken-hearted weeping it was. And Prosper's face was drawn by pity of her. That story of her life and love, it was a sort of saga, something as moving as an old ballad most beautifully sung. He half-guessed then that she had genius; at least, he admitted that it was something more than just her beauty and her sorrow that so greatly stirred him. To speak such sentences in such a voice — that was a gift. She had no more need of words than had a symphony. The varied and vibrant cadences of her voice gave every delicate shading of feeling, of thought. She was utterly expressive. All night, after he had seen her eat and sent her to her bed, the phrases of her music kept repeating themselves in his ears. "An' so I first knowed what lovin' might be like"; and, "I would love you, only somethin' makes me shake away from you — because Pierre's dead." This was a Joan he had not yet realized, and he knew that after all his enchanted leopardess was a woman and that his wooing of her had hardly yet begun. So did she baffle him by the utter directness of her heart. There was so little of a barrier against him and yet — there was so much. For the first time, he doubted his wizardry, and, at that, his desire for the wild girl's love stood up like a giant and gripped his soul.

Joan slept deeply without dreams; she had confessed herself. But Prosper was as restless and troubled as a youth. She had not made her escape; she had followed him home with humility, with confusion in her eyes. She had been glad to hold out her hands again to the fire on his hearth. And yet — he was now her prisoner.

CHAPTER XV

NERVES AND INTUITION

"MR. GAEL," said Joan standing before him at the breakfast-table, "I'm a-goin' to work."

She was pale, gaunt, and imperturbable. He gave her a quick look, one that turned to amusement, for Joan was really as appealing to his humor as a child. She had such immense gravity, such intensity over her one-syllable statements of fact. She announced this decision and sat down.

"Woman's work?" he asked her, smiling quizzically.

"No, sir," with her own rare smile; "I ain't rightly fitted for that."

"Certainly not in those clothes," he murmured crossly, for she was dressed again in her own things.

"I'm a-goin' to do man's work. I'm a-goin' to shovel snow an' help fetch wood an' kerry in water. You tell your Chinese man, please."

"And you're not going to read or study any more?"

"Yes, sir. I like that. If you still want to teach me, Mr. Gael. But I'm a-goin' — I'm *going* — to get some action. I'll just die if I don't. Why, I'm so poor I can't hardly lift a broom. I don't know why I'm so miserably poor, Mr. Gael."

She twisted her brows anxiously.

"You've had a nervous breakdown."

"A *what?*"

"A nervous breakdown."

He lit his cigarette and watched her in his usual lazy, smoke-veiled manner, but she might have noticed the shaken fabric of his self-assurance.

"Say, now," said Joan, "what's that the name for?"

"There's a book about it over there — third volume on the top shelf — look up your case."

With an air of profound alarm, she went over and took it out.

"There's books about everything, ain't there? — is n't there, — Mr. Gael? Why, there's books about lovin' an' about sickness an' about cattle an' what-not, an' about women an' children —" She was shirking the knowledge of her "case," but at last she pressed her lips together and opened the book. She fell to reading, growing anxiety possessed her face, she sat down on the nearest chair, she turned page after page. Suddenly she gave him a look of anger.

"I ain't none of this, Mr. Gael," she said, smote the page, rose with dignity, and returned the book.

He laughed so long and heartily that she was at last forced to join him. "You was — you were — jobbin' me, was n't you?" she said, sighing relief. "Did you know what that volume said? It said like this — I'll read you about it —" She took the volume, found the place and read in a low tone of horror, he helping her with the hard words: "'One of the most frequent forms of phobia, common in cases of psychic neurasthenia, is agrophobia in which patients the moment they come into an open space are oppressed by an exaggerated feeling of anxiety. They may break into a profuse perspiration and assert that they feel as if chained to the ground . . .' And here, listen to this, 'batophobia, the fear that high things will fall, atrophobia, fear of thunder and lightning, pantophobia, the fear of every thing and every one' . . . Well, now, ain't that too awful? An' you mean folks really get that way?"

Their talk was for some time of nervous diseases, Joan's horror increasing.

"Well, sir," said she, "lead me out an' shoot me if I get anyways like that! I believe it's caused by all that queer dressin' an' what-not. I feel like somethin' *real* to-day in this shirt an' all, an' when I get through some work I'll feel a whole lot better. Don't you say I'm one of those nervous breakdowns again, though, will you?" she pleaded.

"No, I won't, Joan. But don't make one of me, will you?"

"How's that?"

"By wearing those clothes all day and half the night. If you expect me to teach you, you'll have to do something for me, to make up for running away. You might put on pretty things for dinner, don't you think? Your nervous system could stand that?"

"My nervous system," drawled Joan, and added startlingly, for she did not often swear, "God!" It was an oath of scorn, and again Prosper laughed.

But he heard with a sort of terror the sound of her "man's work" to which she energetically applied herself. It meant the return of her strength, of her independence. It meant the shortening of her captivity. Before long spring would rush up the cañon in a wave of melting snow, crested with dazzling green, and the valley would lie open to Joan. She would go unless — had he really failed so utterly to touch her heart? Was she without passion, this woman with the deep, savage eyes, the lips, so sensuous and pure, the body so magnificently made for living? She was not defended by any training, she had no moral standards, no prejudices, none of the "ideals." She was completely open to approach, a savage. If he failed, it was a personal failure. Perhaps he had been too subtle, too restrained. She did not yet know, perhaps, what he desired of her. But he was afraid of rousing her hatred, which would be fully as simple and as savage as her love. That evening, after she had dressed to please him, and sat in her chair, tired, but with the beautiful, clean look of outdoor weariness on her face, and tried, battling with drowsiness, to give her mind to his reading and his talk, he was overmastered by his longing and came to her and knelt down, drawing down her hands to him, pressing his forehead on them.

For a moment she was stiff and still, then, "What is it, Mr. Gael?" she asked in a frightened half-voice.

He felt, through her body, the slight recoil of spirit, and drew away, and arose to his feet.

"You're angry?"

He laughed.

"Oh, no. I'm not angry; why should I be? I'm a superman. I'm made — let's say — of alabaster. Women with great eyes and wonderful voices and the beauty of broad-browed nymphs walking gravely down under forest arches, such women give me only a great, great longing to read aloud very slowly and carefully a 'Child's History of the English Race'!" He took the book, tossed it across the room, then stood, ashamed and defiant, laughing a little, a boy in disgrace.

Joan looked at him in profound bewilderment and dawning distress.

"Now," she said, "you *are* angry with me. You always are when you talk that queer way. Won't you please explain it to me, Mr. Gael?"

"No!" said he sharply. "I won't." And he added after a moment, "You'd better go to bed. You're sleepy and as stupid as an owl."

"Oh!"

"Yes. And you've destroyed what little superstitious belief I had left concerning something they tell little ignorant boys about a woman's intuition. You have n't got a bit. You're stupid and I'm tired of you — No, Joan, I'm not.

Don't mind me. I'm only in fun. Please! Damn! I've hurt your feelings."

Her lips were quivering, her eyes full. "I try so awful hard," she said. It was a lovely, broken trail of music.

He bent over her and patted her shoulder. "Dear child! Joan, I won't be so disagreeable again. Only, don't you ever think of me?"

"Yes, yes; all the while I'm thinking of you. I wisht I could do more for you. Why do I make you so angry? I know I'm awful — awfully stupid and ignorant. I — I must drive you most crazy, but truly" — here she turned quickly in his arm and put her hands about his neck and laid her cheek against his shoulder — "truly, Mr. Gael, I'm awful fond of you." Then she drew quickly away, quivered back into the other corner of her great chair, put her face to her hands. "Only — I can't help seein' — Pierre."

Just her tone showed him that still and ghastly youth, and again he saw the brown hand that moved. He had stood between her and that sight. The man ought to have died. He did not deserve his life nor this love of hers. Even though he had failed to kill the man, he would not fail to kill her love for him, sooner or later, thought Prosper. If only the hateful spring would give him time.

He must move her from her memory. She had put her hands about his neck, she had laid her head against his shoulder, and, if it had been the action of a child, then she would not have started from him with that sharp memory of Pierre.

CHAPTER XVI

THE TALL CHILD

THERE were times, even now, when Prosper tried to argue himself back into sardonic self-possession. "Pooh!" said his brain, "you were beside yourself over a loss and then you were shut in for months of winter alone with this mountain girl, so naturally you are off your balance." He would school himself while Joan shoveled outdoors. He would try to see her with critical, clear eyes when she strode in. But one look at her and he was bemused again. For now she was at a great height of beauty, vivid with growing strength and purpose, her lips calm and scarlet, her eyes bright and hopeful. In fact, Joan had made her plans. She would wait till spring, partly to get back her full strength, partly to make further progress in her studies, but mostly in order not to hurt this hospitable Prosper Gael. The naïveté of her gratitude, of her delicate consideration for his feelings, which continually triumphed over an instinctive fear, would have filled him with amusement, perhaps with compunction, had he been capable of understanding them. She was truly sorry that she had hurt him by running away. She told herself she would not do that again. In the spring she would make him a speech of thankfulness and of farewell, and then she would tramp back to Pierre's homestead and win and hold Pierre's land. As yet, you see, Prosper entered very little into her conscious life. Somewhere, far down in her, there was a disturbance, a growing doubt, a something vague and troubling. . . . Joan had not learnt to probe her own heart. A sensation was not, or it was. She was puzzled by the feeling Prosper was beginning to cause her, a feeling of miserable complexity; but she was not yet mentally equipped for the confronting of complexity. It was necessary for an emotion to rush at Joan and throw down, as it were, her heart before she recognized it; even then she might not give it a name. She would act, however, and with violence.

So now she planned and worked and grew beautiful with work and planning, while Prosper curbed his passion and worked, too, and his instruments were delicate and deadly and his plans made no account of hers. Every word he read to her, every note he played for her, had its calculated effect. He worked on her subconsciousness, undermining her path, and at nights and in her sleep she grew aware of him.

But even now, in his cool and passionate heart there were moments of reaction, one at last that came near to wrecking his purpose.

"Your clothes are about done for, Joan," Prosper laughed one morning, watching her belt in her tattered shirt; "you'll soon look like Cophetua's beggar maid."

"I'm not quite barefoot yet." She held up a cracked boot.

"Joan —" He hesitated an instant, then got up from his desk, walked to a window, and looked out at the bright morning. The lake was ruffled with wind, the firs tossed, there were patches of brown-needled earth under his window; his eyes were startled by a strip of green where tiny yellow flowers trod on the very edge of the melting drift. The window was open to soft, tingling air that smelt of snow and of sun, of pines, of growing grass, of sap, of little leaf-buds. The birds were in loud chorus. For several minutes Prosper stared and listened.

"What is it, Mr. Gael?" asked Joan patiently.

He started. "Oh," he said without looking at her again, "I was going to tell you that there are a skirt and a sort of coat in — in a closet in the hall. Do you want to use them?"

She went out to look. In five minutes — he had gone back to his work at the desk — he heard her laugh, and, still laughing, she opened the door again.

"Oh, Mr. Gael, were you really thinking that I could wear these? Look."

He turned and looked at her. She had crowded her strong, lithe frame into a brown tweed suit, a world too narrow for her, and she was laughing heartily at herself and had come in to show him the misfit.

"These things, Mr. Gael," she said, — "they must have been made for a tall child."

Prosper had too far tempted his pain, and in her vivid phrase it came to life before him. She had painted a startling picture and he had seen that suit, so small and trim, before.

Joan saw his face grow white, his eyes stared through her. He drew a quick breath and winced away from her, hiding his face in his hands. A moment later he was weeping convulsively, with violence, his head down between his hands. Joan started toward him, but he made a wicked and repellent gesture. She fled into her room and sat, bewildered, on her bed.

All at once the question came to her: for whom had the delicate fabrics been bought, for whom had this suit been made? "It was his wife and she is dead," thought Joan, and very pitifully she took off the suit, laid it and the other things away, and sitting by her window rested her chin in her hands and stared out through the blue pines. Tears ran down her face because she was so sorry for Prosper's pain. And again, thought Joan, she had caused it, she who owed him everything. Yes, she was deeply sorry for Prosper, deeply; her whole heart was stirred. For the first time she had a longing to comfort him with her hands.

For all that day Prosper fled the house and went across the country, now fording a flood of melted snow, now floundering through a drift, now walking on springy sod, unaware of the soft spring, conscious only of a sort of fire in his breast. He suffered and he resented his suffering, and he would have killed his heart if, by so doing, he could have given it peace. And all day he did not once think of Joan, but only of the "tall child" for whom the gay cañon refuge had been built, but who had never set her slim foot upon its threshold. Sunset found him miles away in the foothills of a low, many-folded range across the plain. He was dog tired, so that for very exhaustion his brain had stopped its tormenting work. He lit a fire and sat by it, huddled in his coat, smoking, dozing, not able really to sleep for cold and hunger. The bright stars, flung all about the sky, mildly regarded him. Coyotes mourned their loneliness and hunger near and far, and once, in the broken woods above him, a mountain lion gave its blood-curdling scream. Prosper hated the night and its beautiful desolation, he hated the God that had made this land. He cursed the dawn when it came delicately, spreading a green arc of radiance across the east. And then, as he arose stiffly, stamped out his fire, and started slowly on his way back, he was conscious of a passionate homesickness, not for the old life he had lost, but for his cabin, his bright hearth, his shut-in solitude, his Joan. Very dear and real and human she was, and her laughter had been sweet. He had shocked it to silence, he had repulsed her comforting hands. She had been so innocent of any desire to hurt him. He could not imagine her ever hurting any one, this broad-browed Joan. She was so kind. And now she must be anxious about him. She would have sat up by the fire all night. . . . His eagerness for her slighted comfort gave his lagging steps a certain vigor, the long walk back seemed very long, indeed. Noon was hot, but he found water and by sundown he came to the cañon trail. He wanted Joan as badly now as a hurt child wants its mother. He came, haggard and breathless, to the door, called "Joan," came into the warm little room and found it empty. Wen Ho, to be sure, pattered to meet him.

"Mister Gael been gone a long time, velly long, all night. Wen Ho, he fix bed, fix breakfast — oh, the lady? She gone out yestiddy, not come back. She leave a letter for him, there on the table."

Prosper took it, waved Wen Ho out, and, dropping into the big chair, opened the paper. There was Joan's big handwriting, that he himself had taught her. Before she could only sign her name.

Mister Gael, dere frend, —

You have ben too good to me an it has ben too hard for you to keep me when you were all the wile amissin her an it hurts me to think of how it must have ben terrible hard for you all this winter to see me where you had ben ust to seein her an me wearin her pretty things all the wile. Now dere frend this must not be no more. I will not stay to trouble you. You have ben awful free-hearted. When you come back from your wanderin an tryin to get over your bein so unhappy you will find your house quiet an peaceful an you will not be hurt by me no more. I am not able to say all I am feelin about your goodness an I hev not always ben as kind to you in my thoughts an axions but that has ben my own fault not yours. I want you to beleave this, Mister Gael. I am goin back to Pierre's ranch to work on his land an some day I will be hopin to see you come ridin in an I will keep on learnin as well as I can an mebbe you will not be ashamed of me. I feel awful bad to go but I would feel more bad to stay when it must hurt you so. Respectably

JOAN

There were blistered spots above that pathetic, mistaken signature. The poor girl had meant to sign herself "Respectfully," and somehow that half-broke his heart.

He drank the strong coffee Wen Ho brought for him, two great cups of it, and he ate a piece of broiled elk meat. Then he went out again and walked rapidly down the trail. It was not yet dark; the world was in a soft glow of rose and violet, opalescent lights. The birds were singing in a hundred chantries. And there, through the firs, a sight to stop his heart, Joan came walking toward him, graceful, free, a swinging figure, bareheaded, her rags girded beautifully about her. And up and up to him she came soundlessly over the pine needles and through the wet snow-patches, looking at him steadfastly and tenderly, without a smile. She came and stood before him, still without dropping her sad, grave look.

"Mr. Gael," she said, "I hev come back. I got out yonder an' "— her breast heaved and a sort of terror came into her eyes — "an' the world was awful lonely. There ain't a creature out yonder to care fer me, fer me to care fer. It seemed like as if it was all dead. I could n't abear it."

She put out her hand wistfully asking for pity, but he fell upon his knees and wrapped his hungry arms about her. "Joan," he sobbed, "Joan! Don't leave me. Don't — I could n't bear it!" He looked up at her, his worn face wet with tears. "Don't leave me, Joan! I want you. Don't you understand?"

Her deep gray eyes filled slowly with light, she put a hand on either side of his face and bent her lips to his. "I never thought you'd be wantin' *me*," she said.

CHAPTER XVII

CONCERNING MARRIAGE

AND it was spring-time; these prisoners of frost were beautifully sensitive. They, too, with the lake and the aspens and the earth, the seeds and the beasts, had suffered the season of interment. In such fashion Nature makes possible the fresh undertakings of last summer's reckless prodigals; she drives them into her mock tomb and freezes their hearts — it is a little rest of death — so that they wake like turbulent bacchantes drunk with sleep and with forgetfulness. Love, spring says, is an eternal fact, welcome its new manifestations. Remating bluebirds built their nests near Joan's window; they were not troubled by sad recollections of last year's nests nor the young birds that flew away. It was another life, a resurrection. If they remembered at all, they remembered only the impulses of pleasure; they had somewhere before learned how to love, how to build; the past summers had given practice to their singing little throats and to their rapid wings. No ghosts forbade happiness and no God — man-voiced — saying, because he knew the ugly human aftermaths, hard sayings of "Be ye perfect."

What counsel was theirs for Joan and what had her human mentor taught her? He had taught her in one form or another the beauty of passion and its eternal sinlessness, for that was his sincere belief. By music he had taught her, by musical speech, by the preaching of heathen sage and the wit of modern arguers. He had given her all the moral schooling she had ever had and its golden rule was, "Be ye beautiful and generous." Joan was both beautiful and made for giving, "free-hearted" as she might herself have said, Friday's child as the old rhyme has it, — and to cry out to her with love, saying, "I want you, Joan," was just, sooner or later, to see her turn and bend her head and hold out her arms. Prosper had the reward of patience; his wild leopardess was tamed to his hand and her sweetness made him tender and very merciful.

Their gay, little house stood open all day while they explored the mountains and plunged into the lake, choosing the hot hour of noon. Joan made herself mistress of the house and did her woman's work at last of tidying and beautifying and decking corners with gorgeous branches of blossoms while Prosper worked at his desk. He was happy; the reality of Joan's presence had laid his ghost just as the reality of his had laid hers. His work went on magically and added the glow of successful creation to the glow of satisfied desire. And his sin of deceit troubled him very little, for he had worked out that problem and had decided that Pierre, dead or alive, was unworthy of this mate.

But sometimes in her sleep Joan would start and moan feeling the touch of the white-hot iron on her shoulder. Her hatred of Pierre's cruelty, her resolution to be done with him forever, must have vividly renewed itself in those dreams, for she would cling to Prosper like a frightened child, and wake, trembling, happy to find herself safe in his arms.

So they lived their spring. Wen Ho, the silent and inscrutable, went out of the valley for provisions, and during his absence Joan queened it in the kitchen. She was learning to laugh, to see the absurd, delightful twists of daily living, to mock Prosper's oddities as he mocked hers. She was learning to be a comrade and she was learning better speech and more exquisite ways. It was inevitable that she should learn. Prosper, in these days, spent his whole soul upon her, fed her with music and delight, and he trained her to sing her sagas so that every day her voice gained in power and flexible sweetness. She would sing, since he told her to, her voice beating its wings against the walls of the house or ringing down the cañon in untrammeled flight. Prosper was lost in wonder of her, in a passionate admiration for his own handiwork. He was making, here in this God-forsaken solitude, a thing of marvel; what he was making surely justified the means. Joan's laughable simplicity and directness were the same; they were part of her essence; no civilizing could confuse or disturb them; but she changed, her brain grew, it absorbed material, it attempted adventures. Nowadays Joan sometimes argued, and this filled Prosper with delight, so quaint and logical she was and so skillful.

They were reading out under the firs by the green lip of the lake, when Wen Ho led his pack-horse up the trail. He had been gone a month, for Prosper had sent him out of the valley to a distant town for his supplies. He did n't want the little frontier place to prick up its ears. Wen Ho had ridden by a secret trail back over the range; he had not passed even the ranger station on his way. He called out, and, in the midst of a sentence Joan was reading, Prosper started up.

Joan looked at him smiling. "You're as easily turned away from learning as a boy," she began, and faltered when she saw his face. It was turned eagerly toward the climbing horses, toward the pack, and it was sharp and keen with detached interest, an excitement that had nothing, nothing in the world to do with her.

It was the great bundle of Prosper's mail that first brought home to Joan the awareness of an outside world. She knew that Prosper was a traveled and widely experienced man, but she had not fancied him held to this world by human attachments. Concerning the "tall child" she had not put a question and she still believed her to have been Prosper's wife. But when, leaving her place under the tree, she came into the house and found Prosper feverishly slitting open envelope after envelope, with a pile of papers and magazines, ankle-high, beside him on the floor, she stood aghast.

"What a lot of people must have been writing to you, Prosper!"

He did not hear her. He was greedy of eye and finger-tips, searching written sheet after sheet. He was flushed along the cheek-bones and a little pale about the lips. Joan stood there, her hands hanging, her head bent, staring up and out at him from under her brows. She looked, in this attitude, rather dangerous.

Prosper sped through his mail, made an odd gesture of desperation, sat still a moment staring, his brilliant, green-gray eyes gone dull and blank, then he gave himself a shuddery shake, pulled a small parcel from under the papers, and held it out to Joan. He smiled.

"Something for you, leopardess," he said — he had told her his first impression of her.

She took the box haughtily and walked with it over to her chair. But he came and kissed her.

"Jealous of my mail? You foolish child. What a girl-thing you are! It does n't matter, does it, how we train you or leave you untrained, you 're all alike, you women, under your skins. Open your box and thank me prettily, and leave matters you don't understand alone. That's the way to talk, is n't it?"

She flushed and smiled rather doubtfully, but, at sight of his gift, she forgot everything else for a moment. It was a collar of topaz and emerald set in heavy silver. She was awe-struck by its beauty, and went, after he had fastened it for her, to stand a long while before the glass looking at it. She wore her yellow dress cut into a V at the neck and the jewels rested beautifully at the base of her long, round throat, faintly brown like her face up to the brow. The yellow and the green brought out all the value of her grave, scarlet lips, the soft, even tints of her skin, the dark lights and shadows of her hair and eyes.

"It's beautiful," she said. "It's wonderful. I love it."

All the time very grave and still, she took it off, put it on its box, and laid it on the mantel. Then she went out of doors.

Prosper hurried to the window and saw her walk out to the garden they had made and begin her work. He was puzzled by her manner, but presently shrugged the problem of her mood away and went back to his mail. That night he finished his novel and got it ready for the publisher.

Again Wen Ho, calm and uncomplaining, was sent out over the hill, and again the idyll was renewed, and Joan wore the collar and was almost as happy as before. Only one night she startled Prosper.

"I asked Pierre," she said slowly, after a silence, in her low-pitched voice, "when he was taking me away home, I asked, 'Where are you going?' and he said to me, 'Don't you savvy the answer to that question, Joan?' And, Prosper, I did n't savvy, so he told me and he looked at me sort of hard and stern, 'We're a-goin' to be married, Joan.'"

Prosper and Joan were sitting before the fire, Joan on the bearskin at his feet, he lounging back, long-legged, smoke-veiled, in one of the lacquered chairs. She had been fingering her collar and she kept on fingering it as she spoke and staring straight into the flames, but, at the last, quoting Pierre's words and tone, her voice and face quivered and she looked at him with eyes of mysterious pain, in them a sort of uncomprehended anguish.

"Why was that, Prosper?" she asked; "I mean, why did he say it that way? And what — what does it stand for, marrying or not —?"

Prosper jerked a little in his chair, then said he blasphemously, "Marriage is the sin against the Holy Ghost. Don't be the conventional woman, Joan. Is n't this beautiful, this life of ours?"

"Yes." But her eyes of uncomprehended pain were still upon him. So he put his hand over them and drew her head against his knee. "Yes, but that other life was — was — before Pierre changed, it was beautiful —"

"Of course. Love is always beautiful. Not even

marriage can always spoil it, though it very often does. Well, Joan," he went on flippantly, though the tickle of her lashes against his palm somehow disturbed his flippancy, "I'll go into the subject with you one of these days, when the weather is n't so beautiful. It's really a matter of law, property rights, and so forth; a practice variously conducted in various lands; it's man's most studied insult to woman; it's recommended as the lesser of two evils by a man who despised woman as only an Oriental can despise her, Saint Paul by name; it's a thing civilized women cry for till they get it and then quite bitterly learn to understand; it's a horrible invention which need n't touch your beautiful clean soul, dear. Come out and look at the moon."

"Listen!" They stood side by side at the door. "Some silly bird thinks that is the dawn. Look at me, Joan!"

She lifted obedient eyes.

"There! That's better. Don't get that other look. I can't bear it. I love you."

A moment later they went out into the sweet, silver silence down to the silver lake.

Four months later the name of Prosper Gael began to be on every one's lips, and before every one's eyes; the world, his world, began to clamor for him. Even Wen Ho grumbled at this going out on tremendous journeys after the mail for which Prosper grew more and more greedy and impatient. His novel, "The Cañon," had been accepted, was enormously advertised, had made an extraordinary success. All this he explained to Joan, who tried to rejoice because she saw that it was exquisite delight to Prosper. He was by way of thinking now that his exile, his Wyoming adventure, was to thank for his success, but when a woman, even such a woman as Joan, begins to feel that she has been a useful emotional experience, there begins pain. For Joan pain began and daily it increased. It was suffering for her to watch Prosper reading his letters, forwarded to him from the Western town where his friends and his secretary believed him to be recovering from some nervous illness; to watch him smoking and thinking of himself, his fame, his talents, his future; to watch him scribbling notes, planning another work, to hear his excited talk, now so impersonal, so unrelated to her; to see how his eagerness over her education slackened, faltered, died; to notice that he no longer watched the changeful humors of her beauty nor cared if she wore bronze or blue or yellow; and worst of all, to find him staring at her sometimes with a worried, impatient look which scuttled out of sight like some ugly, many-legged creature when it met her own eyes — painful, of course, yet such an old story. Joan, who had never heard of such experience, did not foresee the inevitable end, and, in so much, she was spared. The extra pain of forfeiting her dignity and self-respect did not touch her, for she made none of those most pitiful, unavailing efforts to hold him, to cling; did not even pretend indifference. She only drew gradually into herself, shrinking from her pain and from him as the cause of it; she only lost her glow of love-happiness, her face seemed dwindled, seemed to contract, and that secret look of a wild animal returned to her gray eyes. She quietly gave up the old regulations of their life; she did not remind him of the study-hours, the music-hours, the hours of wild outdoor play. She read under the firs, alone; she studied faithfully, alone; she climbed and swam, alone — or with his absent-minded, fitful company; she worked in her garden, alone. At night, when he was asleep, she lay with her hand pressed against her heart, staring at the darkness, listening to the night, waiting. Curiously enough, his inevitable returns of passion and interest, the always decreasing flood-mark, each time a line lower, did not deceive her, did not distract her. She never expressed her trouble, even to herself. She did not give it any words. She took her pain without wincing, without complaint, and when he seemed to need her in any little way, in any big way, she gave because she could not help it, because she had promised him largesse, because it was her nature to give. Besides, although she was instinctively waiting, she did not foresee the end.

It was in late October when, somewhere in the pile of Prosper's mail, there lay a small gray envelope. Joan drew his attention to it, calling it a "queer little letter," and he took it up slowly as though his deft and nervous fingers had gone numb. Before he opened it he looked at Joan and, in one sense, it was the last time he ever did look at her; for at that moment his stark spirit looked straight into hers, acknowledged its guilt, and bade her a mute and remorseful farewell.

He read and Joan watched. His face grew pale and bright as though some electric current had been turned into his veins; his eyes, looking up from the writing, but not returning to her, had the look given by some drug which is meant to stupefy, but which taken in an overdose intoxi-

JOAN WATCHED

cates. He turned and made for the door, holding the little gray folded paper in his hand. On the threshold he half-faced her without lifting his eyes.

"I have had extraordinary news, Joan. I shall have to go off alone and think things out. I don't know when I shall get back." He went out and shut the door gently.

Joan stood listening. She heard him go along the passage and through the second door. She heard his feet on the mountain trail. Afterwards she went out and stood between the two sentinel firs that had marked the entrance to that snow-tunnel long since disappeared. Now it was a late October day, bright as a bared sword. The flowers of the Indian paint-brush burned like red candle flames everywhere under the firs, the fire-weed blazed, the aspen leaves were laid like little golden tiles against the metallic blue of the sky. The high peak pointed up dizzily and down, down dizzily into the clear emptiness of the lake. This great peak stood there in the glittering stillness of the day. A grouse boomed, but Joan was not startled by the sudden rush of its wings. She felt the sharp weight of that silent mountain in her heart; she might have been buried under it. So she felt it all day while she worked, a desperate, bright day, — hideous in her memory, — and at night she lay waiting. After hours longer than any other hours, the door of her bedroom opened and an oblong of moonlight, as white as paper, fell across the matted floor. Prosper stepped in noiselessly and walked over to her bed. He stood a moment and she heard him swallow.

"You're awake, Joan?"

Her eyes were staring up at him, but she lay still.

"Listen, Joan." He spoke in short sentences, waiting between each for some comment of hers which did not come. "I shall have to go away to-morrow. I shall have to go away for some time. I don't want you to be unhappy. I want you to stay here for a while if you will, for as long as you want to stay. I am leaving you plenty of money. I will write and explain it all very clearly to you. I know that you will understand. Listen." Here he knelt and took her hands, which he found lying cold and stiff under the cover, pressed against her heart. "I have made you happy here in this little house, have n't I, Joan?"

She would not answer even this except by the merest flicker of her eyelids.

"You have trusted me; now, trust me a little longer. My life is very complicated. This beautiful year with you, the year you have given to me, is just a temporary respite from — from all sorts of things. I've taught you a great deal, Joan. I've healed the wound that brute made on your shoulder and in your heart. I've taught you to be beautiful. I've filled your mind with beauty. You are a wonderful woman. You'll live to be grateful to me. Some day you'll tell me so."

Her quiet, curved lips moved. "Are you tellin' me good-bye, Prosper?"

It was impossible to lie to her. He bent his head.

"Yes, Joan."

"Then tell it quick and go out and leave me here to-night."

It was impossible to touch her. She might have been wrapped in white fire. He found that though she had not stirred a finger, his hand had shrunk away from hers. He got to his feet, all the cleverness which all day long he had been weaving like a silk net to catch, to bewilder, to draw away her brain from the anguish of full comprehension, was shriveled. He stood and stared helplessly at her, dumb as a youth. And, obedient, he went out and shut the door, taking the white patch of moonlight with him.

So Joan, having waited, behind an obstinately

locked door, for his departure, came out at noon and found herself in the small, gay house alone.

She sat in one of the lacquered chairs and saw after a long while that the Chinaman was looking at her.

Wen Ho, it seemed, had been given instructions. He was to stay and take care of the house and the lady for as long as she wanted it, or him. Afterwards he was to lock up the house and go. He handed her a large and bulky envelope which Joan took and let lie in her lap.

"You can go to-morrow, Wen Ho," she said.

"You no wait for Mr. Gael come back? He say he come back."

"No. I'm not going to wait. I guess" — here Joan twisted her mouth into a smile — "I'm not one of the waiting kind. I'm a-going back to my own ranch now. It won't seem so awful lonesome, perhaps, as I was thinking last spring that it would."

She touched the envelope without looking at it. "Is this money, Wen Ho?"

"I tink so, lady."

She held it, unopened, out to him.

"I will give it to you, then. I have no need of it."

She stood up.

"I am going out now to climb up this mountain back of the house so's I can see just where I am. I'll come down to-night for dinner and to-morrow after breakfast I'll be going away. You understand?"

"Lady, you mean give me all this money?" babbled the Chinaman.

"Yes," said Joan gravely; "I have no need of it."

She went past him with her swinging step.

She was coming down the mountain-side that evening, very tired, but with the curious, peaceful stillness of heart that comes with an entire acceptance of fate, when she heard the sound of horses' hoofs in the hollow of the cañon. Her heart began to beat to suffocation. She ran to where, standing near a big fir tree, she could look straight down on the trail leading up to Prosper's cabin. Presently the horsemen came in sight—the one that rode first was tall and broad and fair, she could see under his hat-brim his straight nose and firmly modeled chin.

"The sin-buster!" said Joan; then, looking at the other, who rode behind him, she caught at the tree with crooked hands and began to sink slowly to her knees. He was tall and slight, he rode with inimitable grace. As she stared, he took off his sombrero, rested his hand on the saddle-horn, and looked haggardly, eagerly, up the trail toward the house. His face was whiter, thinner, worn by protracted mental pain, but it was the beautiful, living face of Pierre.

Joan shrank back into the shadows of the pines, crouched for a few minutes like a mortally wounded beast, then ran up the mountain-side as though the fire that had once touched her shoulder had eaten its way at last into her heart.

Book Two

THE ESTRAY

Book Two: *The Estray*

CHAPTER I

A WILD CAT

THE Lazy-Y ranch-house, a one-storied building of logs, was built about three sides of a paved court. In the middle of this court stood a well with a high rustic top, and about this well on a certain brilliant July night, a tall man was strolling with his hands behind his back. It was a night of full moon, sailing high, which poured whiteness into the court, making its cobbles embedded in the earth look like milky bubbles and drawing clear-cut shadows of the well-top and the gables and chimneys of the house. The man slowly circled the court beginning close to the walls and narrowing till he made a loop about the well, and then, reversing, worked in widening orbits as far as the walls again. His wife, looking out at him through one of the windows, thought that, in the moonlight, followed by his own squat, active shadow, he looked like a huge spider weaving a web. This effect was heightened by the fact that he never looked up. He was deep in some plan to which it was impossible for her not to believe that the curious pattern of his walk bore some relation.

From the northern wing of the ranch-house, strongly lighted, came a tumult of sound; music, thumping feet, a man's voice chanting couplets:

"Oh, you walk right through and you turn around and swing the girl that finds you,
And you come right back by the same old track and turn the girl behind you."

Some one was directing a quadrille in native fashion. There was much laughter, confusion, and applause. None of this noise disturbed the man. He did not look at the lighted windows. He might really have been a gigantic insect entirely unrelated to the human creatures so noisily near at hand.

A man came round the corner of the house, crossed the square, and, lurching a little, made for the door of the lighted wing. Shortly after his entrance the sound of music and dancing abruptly stopped. This stillness gave the spider pause, but he was about to renew his weaving, when, in the silence, a woman spoke.

"You, Mabel, don't you go home," she said.

She had not spoken loudly, but her voice beat against the walls of the court as though it could have filled the whole moonlight night with dangerous beauty. The listener outside lifted his head with a low, startled exclamation. Suddenly the world was alive with adventure and alarm.

"Mind your own business, you wild cat," answered a man's raucous voice. "She's my wife, which is somethin' that your sort knows nothin' about. Come on, you Mabel. You think that outlaw can keep me from takin' home my wife, you're betting wrong."

Another silence; then the voice again, a little louder, as though the speaker had stepped out into the center of the room.

"Mabel is not a-goin' home with you," it said; and the listener outside threw back his head with the gesture of a man sensitive to music who listens to some ecstatic melody. "She happens to be stoppin' here with us to-night. You say that she's your wife, but that don't mean that she belongs to you, body and soul, Bill Greer — not to you, who don't possess your own body, or soul. Why, you can't keep your feet steady, you can't pull your hand away from mine. You can't hold your tipsy eyes on mine. Do you call that ownin' your own body? And as fer your soul, it's a hell of rage and dirty feelin's that I'd hate to burn my eyes by lookin' closely at."

A deep, short, alarming chorus of laughter interrupted the speech. The speaker evidently had her audience.

"So you don't own anything to-night," went on the extraordinary, deliberate voice; "surely you don't own Mabel. You can't get a claim on her, not thataway. She's her own. She belongs to her own self. When you're fit to take her, why, then come and tell us about it, and if we judge you're a-tellin' us the truth, mebbe we'll let her go. Till then —" a pause which was filled with a rapid shuffling of feet. The door flew open and in its lighted oblong the observer saw a huddled figure behind which rose a woman's black and shapely head. "Till then," repeated the deep-toned, ringing voice, "*get out!*" And the huddled man came on a staggering run which ended in a backward fall on the cobbles of the court.

The man who watched trod lightly past him and came to the open door. Inside, firelight beat on the golden log walls and salmon-colored timber ceiling; a lamp hanging from a beam threw down a strong, conflicting arc of white light. A dozen brown-faced, booted young men stood about, three musicians were ready to take up their interrupted music, the little fat man who had called out the figures of the quadrille, stood on a barrel, his arms folded across his paunch. A fair-haired girl, her face marred by recent tears, drooped near him. Two of the young men were murmuring reassurances to her; others surrounded a stout, red-faced girl who was laughing and talking loudly. The Jew's eyes wandered till they came to the fireplace. There another woman leaned against the wall.

The music struck up, the dancing began again, the two other girls, quickly provided with partners, began to waltz, the superfluous men stood up together and went at it with gravity and grace. No one asked this woman, who stood at ease, watching the dancers, her hands resting on her hips, her head tilted back against the logs. As he looked at her, the intruder had a queer little thrill of fright. He remembered something he had once seen — a tame panther which was to be used in some moving-picture play. Its confident owner had led it in on a chain and held it negligently in a corner of the room, waiting for his cue. The panther had stood there drowsily, its eyes shifting a little, then, watching people, its inky head had begun to move from side to side. He remembered the way the loose chain jerked. The animal's eyes half-closed, it lowered its head, its upper lip began to draw away from its teeth. All at once it had dropped on its belly. Some one cried out, "Hold your beast!"

This young woman by the fireplace had just that panther-air of perilous quietness. She was very haggard, very thin; she wore her massive, black hair drawn away hideously from brow and temple, and out of this lean, unshaded face a pair of deep eyes looked drowsily, dangerously. Her mouth was straightened into an expression of proud bitterness, her round chin thrust forward; there was a deep, scowling line that rose from the bridge of her straight, short nose almost to the roots of her hair. It cut across a splendidly modeled brow. She was very graceful, if such a bundle of bones might be said to have any grace. Her pose was arresting. There was a tragic force and attraction about her.

The man by the door appraised her carefully between his narrowed lids. He kept in mind the remembered melody of her voice, and, after a few moments, he strolled across the floor and came up to her.

"Will you dance?" he said.

He had a very charming and subtle smile, a very charming and sympathetic look. The woman was startled, color rose into her face. She stared at him.

"I'm not dancing, Mr. Morena," she answered.

"You know my name," smiled Morena; "and I don't know yours. I've been on Mr. Yarnall's ranch for a month. Why have n't I seen you?"

"Fer not lookin', I suppose." She had given him that one startled glance, and now she had turned her eyes back to the dancers and wore a grim, contemptuous air. Her speeches, though they were cut into short, crisp words, were full of music of a sharp, metallic quality different from the tone of her other speech, but quite as beautifully expressive.

"May I smoke?" asked Morena. He was still smiling his charming smile and watching her out of the corners of his eyes.

"I'm not hinderin' you any," said she.

Morena smiled deeper. He took some time making and lighting his cigarette.

"You don't smoke, yourself?" he asked.

"No."

"Nor dance?"

"No."

"Nor behave prettily to polite young men?"

Again the woman looked at him. "You ain't so awful young, are you?"

He laughed aloud.

"I amuse you, don't I? Well, I'm not always so all-fired funny," drawled the creature, lowering her head a little.

"No. I've heard that you're not. You rather run things here, I gather; got the boys 'plumb-scared'?"

"Did Mr. Yarnall tell you that?"

"Yes. I've just in the last few minutes remembered who you are. You're Jane. You cook for the 'outfit,' and Yarnall was telling us the other night how he sent one of the boys out for a cook, the last one, a man, having been beaten up, and how the boy had brought you back behind him on his saddle. He said you'd kept order for him ever since, were better than a foreman. Who was the man you threw out to-night?"

"Perhaps," drawled Jane, "he was just a feller who asked too many questions?"

Again Morena's smile deepened into his cheeks. He gave way, in the Jewish fashion so deceptively suggestive of meekness and timidity, when it is, at its worst, merely pliable insolence, at its best, pliable determination. "You must pardon me, Miss Jane," he said in his murmuring, cultivated voice. "You see I've had a great misfortune. I've never been in your West. I've lived in New York where good manners have n't time or space to flourish. I had n't the least intention of being impertinent. Do you want me to go?"

He moved as if to leave her, and she did not lift a finger to detain him.

"I'm not carin'. Do as you please," she said with entire indifference.

"Oh," said Morena, looking back at her, "I don't stay where people are 'not carin'.'"

She gave him an extraordinarily intelligent look. "I should say that's the only place you'd be wantin' to stay in at all — where you're not exactly urged to come," she said.

Morena flushed and his lids flickered. He was for an instant absurdly inclined to anger and made two or three steps away. But he came back.

He bowed and spoke as he would have spoken to a great lady, suavely, deferentially.

"Good-night. I wish I could think that you have enjoyed our talk as greatly as I have, Miss Jane. I should very much like to be allowed to repeat it. May I be stupidly personal and tell you that you are very beautiful?" He bowed, gave her an upward look and went out, finding his way cleverly among the dancers.

Outside, in the moonlit court, he stood, threw back his head and laughed, not loudly but consumedly. He was remembering her white face of mute astonishment. She looked almost as if his compliment had given her sharp pain.

Morena went laughing to his room in the opposite wing. He wanted to describe the interview to his wife.

CHAPTER II

MORENA'S WIFE

BETTY MORENA was sitting in a rustic chair before an open fire, smoking a cigarette. She was a short woman, so slenderly, even narrowly built, as to appear overgrown, and she was a mature woman so immaturely shaped and featured as to appear hardly more than a child. Her curly, russet hair was parted at the side, her wide, long-lashed eyes were set far apart, her nose was really a finely modeled snub, — more, a boy's nose even to a light sprinkling of freckles, — and her mouth was provokingly the soft, red mouth of a sorrowful child. She lounged far down in her chair, her slight legs, clad in riding-breeches of perfect cut, stretched out straight, her limber arms along the arms of the chair, her chin sunk on her flat chest, and her big, clear eyes staring into the fire. It was an odd figure of a wife for Jasper Morena, a Jew of thirty-eight, producer and manager of plays.

When Betty Kane had run away with him, there had been lamentation and rage in the houses of Kane and of Morena. To the pride of an old

Hebrew family, the marriage even of this wandering son with a Gentile was fully as degrading as to the pride of the old Tory family was the marriage with a Jew. Her perverse Gaelic blood on fire with the insults heaped upon her lover, Betty, seventeen years old, romantic, clever, would have walked over flint to give her hand to him. That was ten years ago. Now, when Jasper came into her room, she drew her quick brows together, puffed at her cigarette, and blinked as though she was looking at something distasteful and at the same time rather alarming.

"Have they stopped dancing, Jasper?" she asked in a voice that was at once brusque and soft.

Jasper rubbed his hands delightedly. He was still merry, and came to stand near the fire, looking down at her with eyes entirely kind and admiring.

"Have you ever noticed Jane, who cooks for the outfit, Betty?"

"Yes. She's horrible."

"She's extraordinary, and I mean to get hold of her for Luck's play. Did you read it?"

"Yes."

"The play is absolutely dependent on the leading part and I have found it simply impossible to fill. Now, here's a woman of extraordinary grace and beauty —"

Betty lifted skeptical eyebrows, twisted her limber mouth, but forbore to contradict.

"And with a magical voice — a woman who not only looks the part, but is it. You remember Luck's heroine?"

Betty flicked off the ash of her cigarette and looked away. "A savage, is n't she? The man has her tamed, takes her back to London, and there gives her cause for jealousy and she springs on him — yes, I remember. This woman, Jane, is absolutely without education and has n't a notion of acting, I suppose."

Jasper rubbed his hands with increased delight. "Not a notion and she murders the King's English. But she *is* Luck's savage and — in spite of your eyebrows, Betty — she is beautiful. I can school her. It will take money, no end of patience, but I can do it. It's one of the things I can do. But, of course, there's the initial difficulty of persuading her to try it."

"That ought n't to be any difficulty at all. Of course she'll jump at the chance."

"I'm not so sure. She was ready to throw me out of the kitchen to-night. She is really a virago. Do you know what one of the men said about her?" Jasper laughed and imitated the gentle Western drawl. "Jane 's plumb movin' to me. She's about halfway between 'You go to hell' and 'You take me in your arms to rest.'"

Betty smiled. Her smile was vastly more mature than her appearance. It was clever and cynical and cold. The Oriental, looking down at her, lost his merriment.

"Do you feel better, dear?" he asked timidly. "Do you think you will be able to go back next week?"

She stood up as he came nearer and walked over to the little table that played the part of dressing-table under a wavy mirror. "Oh, yes. I am quite well. I don't think the doctors have much sense. I'm sure I had n't anything like a nervous breakdown. I was just tired out."

Jasper drew back the hand whose touch she had eluded, and nervously, his long supple fingers a little unsteady, lighted a cigarette. At that moment he did not look like a spider, but like a lover who has been hurt. Betty could see in the mirror a distorted image of his dejected gracefulness, but, entirely unmoved, she put up her thin, brown hands and began to take the pins out of her hair.

"I like your Jane experiment," she said. "Let

me know how you get on with it and whether I can help. I shall have to turn in now. I'm dead beat. Yarnall took me halfway up the mountain and back. Good-night."

Jasper looked at her, then pressed his lips into a straight line and went to the door which led from her bedroom to his. He said "Good-night" in a low tone, glanced at her over his shoulder, and went out.

Betty waited an instant, then slowly unlaced her heavy, knee-high boots, took them off, and began to walk to and fro on stocking feet, hands clasped behind her back. With her curly hair all about her face and shoulders, she looked like a wild, extravagantly naughty school-girl, a girl in a wicked temper, a rebel against authority. In fact, she was rejoicing that this horrible enforced visit to the West was all but over. One week more! She was almost at an end of her endurance. How she hated the beautiful white night outside, those mountain peaks, the sound of that rapid river, the stillness of sagebrush, the voice of the big pines! And she hated the log room, its simplicity now all littered with incongruous luxuries; ivory toilet articles on the board table; lacy, beribboned underwear thrown over the rustic chair; silver-framed photographs; an exquisite, gold-mounted crystal vase full of wild flowers on the pine shelf; satin bedroom slippers on the clay hearth; a gorgeous, fur-trimmed dressing-gown over the foot of her narrow, iron cot; all the ridiculous necessities that Betty's maid had put into her trunk. Yes, Betty hated it all because it was what she had always thirsted for. What a malevolent trick of fate that Jasper should have brought her to Wyoming, that the doctor had insisted upon at least a month of just this life. "Take her West," he had said, and Betty, lying limp and white in her bed, her small head sunk into the pillow, had jerked from head to foot. "Take her West. I know a ranch in Wyoming — Yarnall's. She'll get outdoor exercise, tonic air, sound sleep, release from all these pestiferous details, like a cloud of flies, that sting women's nerves to death. Don't pay any attention to whether she likes it or not. Let her behave like a naughty child, let her kick and scream and cry. Pick her up, Morena, and carry her off. Do you hear? Don't let her make you change your plans." The doctor had seen his patient's convulsive jerk. "Pack her up. Make your reservations and go straight to 'Buck' Yarnall's ranch, Lazy-Y, — that's his brand, I believe, — Middle Fork, Wyoming. I'll send him a wire. He knows me.

She needs all outdoors to run about in. She needs joggin' around all day through the sagebrush on a cow-pony in that sun; she needs the smell of a camp-fire — Gad! wish I could get back to it myself."

Betty, having heard this out, began to laugh. She laughed till they gave her something to keep her quiet. But, except for that laughter, she had made no protest whatever; she did not "kick and scream and cry." In fact, though she looked like a child, she was not at all inclined to such exhibitions. This doctor had not seen her through her recent ordeal. Two years before her breakdown, Jasper had been terribly hurt in an automobile accident, and Betty had come to him at the hospital, had waited, as white as a snow-image, for the result of the examination. They had told her emphatically that there was no hope. Jasper Morena could not live for more than a few days. She must not allow herself to hope. He might or might not regain consciousness. If he did, it would be for a few minutes before the end. Betty had listened with her white, rigid, child face, had thanked them, had gone home. There in her exquisite, little sitting room above Central Park, she had sat at her desk and written a few lines on square, gray note paper.

"Jasper is dying," she had written. "By the time you get this, he will be dead. If you can forgive me for having failed in courage last year, come back. What I have been to you before I will be again, only, this time we can love openly. Come back."

Then she had dropped her head on the desk and cried. Afterwards she had addressed her letter to a certain Prosper Gael. The letter went to Wyoming. When it reached its destination, it was taken over a mountain-range by a patient Chinaman.

Three days later Jasper regained consciousness and began slowly to return to health. He had the tenacious vitality of his race, and, in his own spirit, an iron will to live. He kept Betty beside his bed for hours, and held her cold hand in his long, sensitive one, and he stared at her under his lashes till she thought she must go mad. But she did not. She nursed him through an interminable convalescence. She received Prosper, very early in this convalescence, by her husband's bed, and Jasper had murmured gratitude for the emotion that threatened to overwhelm his friend. It was not till some time — an extraordinarily long time — after Morena's complete recovery that she had snapped like a broken icicle. And then, forsooth, they had sent her to Wyoming to get back her health!

Having paced away some of her restlessness, Betty stopped by the cabin window and pushed aside one of the short, calico curtains. She looked out on the court. A tall woman had just pulled up a bucket of water from the well and had emptied it into a pitcher. She finished, let the bucket drop with a whirr and a clash, and raised her head. For a second she and Jasper Morena's wife looked at each other. Betty nodded, smiled, and drew the curtain close.

CHAPTER III

JANE

AFTER that night, there began a sort of persecution, skillfully conducted by Jasper and Betty, against the ferocity of Jane. It was a persecution impossible to imagine in any other setting, even the social simplicity of Lazy-Y found itself a trifle amused. For Jasper, the stately Jewish figure, would carry pails of water for Jane from the well to the kitchen, would help her in the vegetable garden, and to straighten out her recalcitrant stove-pipe; Betty would put on an apron a mile too large, to wash dishes and shell peas. She would sit on the kitchen table swinging her long, childlike legs and chatter amiably. Jasper talked, too, to the virago, talked delightfully, about horses and dogs, — he had a charming gift of humorous observation, — talked about hunting and big-game shooting, about trapping, about travel, and, at last, about plays. Undoubtedly Jane listened. Sometimes she laughed. Once in a while she ejaculated, musically, "Well!" Occasionally she swore.

One afternoon he met her riding home from

an errand to a neighboring ranch, and, turning his horse, rode with her. In worn corduroy skirt, flannel shirt, and gray sombrero, she looked like a handsome, haggard boy, and, that afternoon, there was a certain unusual wistfulness in her eyes, and her mouth had relaxed a little from its bitterness. Perhaps it was the beauty of a clear, keen summer day; without doubt, also, she was touched by the courteous pleasure of his greeting and by his giving up his ride in order to accompany her. She even unbent from her silence and, for the first time, really talked to him. And she spoke, too, in a new manner, using her beautiful voice with beautiful carefulness. It was like a master-musician who, after a long illness, takes up his beloved instrument and tentatively tests his shaken powers. Jasper had much ado to keep his surprise to himself, for the rough ranch girl could speak pure enough English if she would.

"You and your wife are leaving soon?" she asked him, and, when he nodded, she gave a sigh. "I'll be missing you," she said, throwing away her *brusquerie* like a rag with which she was done. "You've been company for me. You've made use of lots of patience and courage, but I have really liked it. I've not got the ways of being sociable and I don't know that I want ever to get them. I am not seeking for friends. There is n't another person on the ranch that would dare talk to me as you and Mrs. Morena have talked. They don't know anything about me here and I don't mean that they should know." She paused, then gave way to an impulse of confidence. "One of the boys asked me to marry him. He came and shouted it through the window and I caught him with a pan of water." She sighed. "I don't know rightly if he meant it for a joke or not, but the laugh was n't on me."

Jasper controlled his laughter, then saw the dry humor of her eyes and lips and let out his mirth.

"Why, sir," said Jane, "you'd be surprised at the foolishness of men. Sometimes it seems that, just for pure contrariness, they want to marry her that least wants them about. The day I came tramping into this valley, I stopped for food at the ranch of an old bachelor down yonder at the ford. And he invited me to be his wife while I was drinking a glass of water from his well. He told me how much money he had and said he'd start my stove for me winter mornings. There's a good husband! And he was sure kind to me even when I told him 'no.' 'T was that same evening that the boy from Lazy-Y rode in and claimed me for a cook. Mr. Yarnall is a trusting man. He took me and did n't ask any questions. I told him I was 'Jane' and that I was n't planning to let him know more. He has n't asked me another question since. He's a gentleman, I figure it, and he's kind of quiet himself about what he was before he came to this country. He's a man of fifty and he has lots back of him only he's taken a fresh start." She sighed, "Folks like you and Betty seem awfully open-hearted. It's living in cities, I suppose, where every one knows every one else so well."

This astonishing picture of the candid simplicity of New York's social life absorbed Jasper's attention for some time.

"Would n't you like to live in a city, Jane?"

She laughed her short, boyish "Hoo!" "It is n't what I would like, Mr. Morena," she said. "Why, I'd like to see the world. I would like to be that fellow who was condemned to wander all over the earth and never to die. He was a Jew, too, was n't he?"

Jasper flushed. People were not in the habit of making direct reference to his nationality, and, being an Israelite who had early cut himself off with dislike from his own people and cultivated the society of Gentiles, "a man without a country," he was acutely sensitive.

"The Wandering Jew? Yes. Where did you ever hear of him?"

"I read his story," she answered absently; "an awful long one, but interesting, about lots of people, by Eugène Sue."

Jasper's lips fell apart and he stared. She had spoken unwittingly and he could see that she was not thinking of him, that she was far away, staring beyond her horse's head into the broad, sunset-brightened west.

"Where were you schooled?" he asked her.

He had brought her back and her face stiffened. She gave him a startled, almost angry look, dug her heels into her horse and broke into a gallop; nor could he win from her another word.

A few days before he left, he took Yarnall into his confidence. At first the rancher would do nothing but laugh. "Jane on the boards! That's a notion!" followed by explosion after explosion of mirth. The Jew waited, patient, pliant, smiling, and then enumerated his reasons. He talked to Yarnall for an hour, at the end of which time, Yarnall, his eyes still twinkling, sent for Jane.

The two men sat in a log-walled room, known as the office. Yarnall's big desk crowded a stove. There was no other furniture except shelves and a box seat beneath a window. Jasper sat on the end of the desk, swinging his slim, well-booted leg; Yarnall, stocky, gray, shabby, weather-beaten, leaned back in his wicker chair. The door which Jasper faced was directly behind Yarnall. When Jane opened it, he turned.

The girl looked grim and a little pale. She was evidently frightened. This summons from Yarnall suggested dismissal or reproof. She came around to face him and stood there, looking fierce and graceful, her head lowered, staring gloomily at him from under her brows. To Jasper she gave not so much as a glance.

"Well, Jane, I fancy I shall have to let you go," said Yarnall. He was not above tormenting the wild-cat. Female ferocity always excites the teasing boy in a man. "You 're getting too ambitious for us. You see, once these rich New Yorkers take you up, you 're no more use to a plain ranchman like me."

"What are you drivin' at?" asked Jane.

"Do let me explain it to her, Yarnall!" Jasper snapped his elastic fingers, color had risen to his face, and he looked annoyed. "Miss Jane, won't you sit down?"

Jane turned her deep, indignant eyes upon him. "Are you and your wife the rich New Yorkers he says are takin' me up?"

"No, no. He's joking. This is a serious business. It's of vital importance to me and it ought to be of vital importance to you. Please do sit down!"

Jane took a long step back and sat down on the settle under the long, horizontal window. She folded her hands on her knee and looked up at Morena. She had transferred her attention completely to him. Yarnall watched them. He was an Englishman of much experience and this picture of the skillful, cultivated, handsome Jew angling deftly for the gaunt, young savage diverted him hugely. He screwed up his eyes to get a picture of it.

"I am a producer and manager of plays," said Jasper, "which means that I take a play written by a more gifted man and arrange it for the stage. Have you ever seen a play?"

"No, sir."

"But you have some idea what they are?"

"Yes. I have read them. Shakespeare wrote quite a lot of that kind of talking pieces, did n't he?"

Jasper was less surprised than Yarnall. "At present I have a play on my hands which is a very brilliant and promising piece of work, but which I have been unable to produce for lack of a heroine. There is n't an actress on my list that can take the part and do it justice. Now, Miss Jane, I believe that with some training you could take it to perfection. My wife and I would like to take you to New York, paying all your expenses, of course, and put you into training at once. It would take a year's hard work to get you fitted for the part. Then next fall we could bring out the play and I think I can promise you success and fame and wealth in no small measure. I don't know you very well; I don't know whether or not you are ambitious; but I do know that every woman must love beauty and ease and knowledge and experience. For what else," he smiled, "did Eve eat the apple? All these you can have if you will let us take you East. Of course, if I find you cannot take this part, I will hold myself accountable for you. I will not let you be a loser in any way by the experiment. With your beauty" — Yarnall fell back in his chair and gaped from the excited speaker to the silent listener — "and your extraordinary voice, and your magnetism, you must be especially fitted for a career of some kind. I promise to find you your career."

Every drop of blood had fallen from Jane's face and the rough hands on her knee were locked together.

"What part," she asked in a quick, low voice, "is this that you think I could learn to do?"

Jasper changed his position. He came nearer and spoke more rapidly. "It is the story of a girl, a savage girl, whom a man takes up and trains. He trains her as a professional might train a lioness. It is a passion with him to break spirits and shape them to his will. He trains her with coaxing and lashing — not actual lashing, though I believe in one place he does come near to beating her — and he gets her broken so that she lies at his feet and eats out of his hand. All this, you understand, while he's an exile from his own world. Then, in the second act, — that is the second part of the play, — he takes his tamed lioness back to civilization. They go to London and there the woman does his training infinite credit. She is extraordinarily beautiful; she is civilized, successful, courted. Her eccentricities only add to her charm. So it goes on very prettily for a while. Then he makes a mistake. He blunders very badly. He gives his lioness cause for jealousy and — to come to the point — she flies at his throat. You see, he had n't really tamed her. She was under the skin, a lioness, a beast, at heart."

Jasper had been absorbed in the plot and had

not noticed Jane, but Yarnall for several minutes had been leaning forward, his hands tightened on the arms of his chair. The instant Jasper stopped he held up his hand.

"Quiet, Jane," he said softly as a man might speak to a plunging horse. "Steady!"

Jane got to her feet. She was very white. She put up her hand and pressed the back of it against her forehead and from under this hand she looked at the two men with eyes of such astonished pain and beauty as they could never forget.

"Yes," she said presently; "that's something I *could* do."

At once Jasper hastened to retrieve his error. "Oh, I'm so sorry. I've been horribly clumsy. Do forgive me. Do let me explain. I did n't mean that you were a wild —"

She let the hand fall and held it up to stop his speech. "I'm not taking offense, Mr. Morena," she said. "You say you arrange plays and that you have been seeking for some one to play that girl, that lioness-girl who was n't rightly tamed, though the man had done his worst to break her?"

Jasper nodded with a puzzled, anxious air. For all his skill and subtlety, he could not interpret her tone.

"And you think I'm beautiful?"

"My dear child, I know you are," said he. "You try to disguise it. And I know that in many other ways you disguise yourself. I think you make a great mistake. Your work is hard and rough —"

She smiled. "I'm not complaining of my work," she said. "It's rough and so am I. Oh, yes, I'm real, true rough. I was born to roughness and raised to it. I'm not anything I don't seem, Mr. Morena. I've had rough travel all my days, only — only —" She sat down again, twisting her hands painfully in her apron and bending her face down from the sight of the two men. The line of her long, bent neck was a beautiful thing to see. She spoke low and rapidly, holding down her emotion, though she could not control all the exquisite modulations of her voice. "There's only one part of my travel that I want to forget and that's the one smooth bit. And it's hateful to me and you've been reminding me of it. I must tell you now that I'd rather be burnt by a white-hot iron" — here she gave him a wide and horrified look like a child who speaks of some dreadful remembered punishment — "than do that thing you've asked of me. I hate everything you've been telling me about. I don't want to be beautiful. I don't want any one to be telling me such things. I don't want to be any different from what I am now. This is my real self. It is. I hate beauty. I hate it. I'm not good enough to love it. Beauty and learning and—and music—"

Her head had been bending lower and lower, her voice rocking under its weight of restrained anguish. On the word "music" she dropped her head to her knees and was silent.

"I can't talk no more," she said, after a moment, and she stood up and ran out of the room.

"I'll be d——d!" swore Yarnall.

But Jasper stood, his face pale, smiting one hand into the other.

"I feel that I, at least, deserve to be," he said.

CHAPTER IV

FLIGHT

THERE was a girl named Joan who followed Pierre Landis because he laid his hand upon her wrist, and there was another Joan who fled up the mountain-side at sight of him, as though the fire that had once touched her shoulder had burnt its way into her heart. Then there was a third Joan, a Joan astray. It was this Joan that had come to Lazy-Y Ranch and had cooked for and bullied "the outfit" — a Joan of set face and bitter tongue, whose two years' lonely battle with life had twisted her youth out of its first comely straightness. In Joan's brief code of moral law there was one sin — the dealings of a married woman with another man. When Pierre's living and seeking face looked up toward her where she stood on the mountain-side above Prosper's cabin, she felt for the first time that she had sinned, and so, for the first time, she was a sinner, and the inevitable agony of soul began.

She fled and hid till dark, then prowled about till she knew that Wen Ho was alone in the house. She came like a spirit from hell and questioned him.

"What did the men ask? What did you tell them?"

The men had asked for a lady. He had told them, as Prosper had once instructed him, that no lady was living there, that the man had just gone. They had been satisfied and had left. But Joan was still in terror. Pierre must never find her now. She had accepted the lie of a stranger, had left her husband for dead, had made no effort to ascertain the truth, and had "dealings with another man." Joan sat in judgment and condemned herself to loneliness. She turned herself out from all her old life as though she had been Cain, and, following Wen Ho's trail over the mountains, had gone into strange lands to work for her bread. She called herself "Jane" and her ferocity was the armor for her beauty. Always she worked in fear of Pierre's arrival, and, as soon as she had saved money enough for further traveling, she moved on. She worked by preference on lonely ranches as cook or harvester, and it was after two years of such life that she had drifted into Yarnall's kitchen. She was then greatly changed, as a woman who works to the full stretch of her strength, who suffers privation and hardship, who gives no thought to her own youth and beauty, and who, moreover, suffers under a scourge of self-scorn and fear, is bound to change. Of all the people that had seen her after months of such living, Jasper Morena was the only one to find her beautiful. But with his sensitive observation he had seen through the shell to the sweetness underneath; for surely Joan was sweet, a Friday's child. It was good that Jasper had torn the skin from her wound, good that he had broken up the hardness of her heart. She left him and Yarnall that afternoon and went away to her cabin in the trees and lay face down on the bare boards of the floor and was young again. Waves of longing for love and beauty and adventure flooded her. For a while she had been very beautiful and had been very passionately loved; for a while she had been surrounded by beauty and taught its meanings. She had fled from it all. She hated it, yes, but she longed for it with every fiber of her being. The last two years were scalded away. She was Joan, who had loved Pierre; Joan, whom Prosper Gael had loved.

Toward morning, dawn feeling with white fingers through the pine boughs into her uncurtained window, Joan stopped her weeping and stood up. She was very tired and felt as though all the hardness and strength had been beaten from her heart. She opened her door and looked at pale stars and a still, slowly brightening world. In a hollow below the pines a stream ran and poured its hoarse, hurrying voice into the silence. Joan bent under the branches, undressed and bathed. The icy water shocked life back into her spirit. She began to tingle and to glow. In spite of herself she felt happier. She had been stony for so long, neither sorrowful nor glad; now, after the night of sharp pain, she was aware of the gladness of morning. She came up from her plunge, glowing and beautiful, with loose, wet hair.

In the corral the men were watering their teams; above them on the edge of a mesa, against the rosy sky, the other ponies, out all night on the range, were trooping, driven by a cowboy who darted here and there on his nimble pony, giving shrill cries. In the clear air every syllable was sharp to the ear, every tint and line sharp to the eye. It was beautiful, very beautiful, and it was near and dear to her, native to her — this loveliness of quick action, of inarticulate calling to dumb beasts, of work, of simple, often repeated beginnings. She was glad that she was working with her hands. She twisted up her hair and went over to the ranch-house where she began soberly and thankfully to light her kitchen fire.

It was after breakfast, two or three mornings later, when a stranger on a chestnut pony rode into Yarnall's ranch, tied his pony to a tree, and, striding across the cobbled square, came to knock at the office door. At the moment, Yarnall, on the other side of the house, was saying farewell to his guests, and helping the men pile the baggage into the two-seated wagon, so this other visitor, getting no answer to his knock, turned and looked about the court. He did not, it was evident, mind waiting. It was to be surmised from the look of him that he was used to it; patient and not to be discouraged by delay. He was a very brown young man of quite astounding beauty and his face had been schooled to keenness and restraint. He was well-dressed, very clean, an outdoor man, a rider, but a man who had, in some sense, arrived. He had the inimitable stamp of achievement. He had been hard driven — the look of that, too, was there; he had been driven to more than ordinary effort. One of the men, seeing him, walked over and spoke respectfully.

"You want to see Mr. Yarnall?"

THE STRANGER DROPPED TO HIS HEELS, SQUATTED, AND ROLLED A CIGARETTE

"Yes, sir." The man's eyes were searching the ranch-house wistfully again. "I would like to see him if I can. I have some questions to ask him."

"He's round the house, gettin' rid of a bunch of dudes. Some job. Both hands tied up. Will you go round or wait?"

The stranger dropped to his heels, squatted, and rolled a cigarette.

"I'll wait," he murmured. "You can let him know when the dudes make their get-away. He'll get round to me. My name? It won't mean anything to him — Pierre Landis."

He did not go round the house, and Yarnall, being very busy and perturbed for some time after the departure of his guests, did not get round to him till nearly noon. By that time he was sitting on the step, his back against the wall, still smoking and still wistfully observant of his surroundings.

He stood up when Yarnall came.

"Sorry," said the latter; "that fool boy did n't tell me you were here till ten minutes ago. Come in. You'll stop for dinner — if we get any to-day."

"Thank you," said Pierre.

He came in and talked and stayed for dinner. Yarnall was used to the Western fashion of doing business. He knew that it would be a long time before the young man would come to his point. But the Englishman was in no hurry, for he liked his visitor and found his talk diverting enough. Landis had been in Alaska — a lumber camp. He had risen to be foreman and now he was off for a vacation, but had to go back soon. He had been everywhere. It seemed to Yarnall that the stranger had visited every ranch in the Rocky Mountain belt.

After dinner, strolling beside his host toward his horse, Pierre spoke, and before Yarnall had heard a word he knew that the long delay had been caused by suppressed emotion. Pierre, when he did ask his question, was white to the lips.

"I've taken a lot of your time," he said slowly. "I came to ask you about some one. I heard that you had a woman on your ranch, a woman who came in and did n't give you any history. I want to see her if I may." He was actually fighting an unevenness of breath, and Yarnall, unemotional as he was, was gripped with sympathetic suspense. "I want," stammered the young man, "to know her name."

Yarnall swore. "Her name, as she gave it," said he, "is Jane. But, my boy, you can't see her. She left this morning."

Pierre raised a white, tense face.

"Left?" He turned as if he would run after her.

"Yes, sir. These people I've had here took her away with them. That is, they've been urging her to go, but she'd refused. Then, suddenly, this morning, just as they were putting the trunks in, up came Jane, white as chalk, asking them to take her with them, said she must go. Well, sir, they rigged her up with some traveling clothes and drove away with her. That was six hours ago. By now they're in the train, bound for New York."

Yarnall's guest looked at him without speaking, and Yarnall nervously went on, "She's been with us about six months, Landis, and I don't know anything about her. She was tall, gray eyes, black hair, slow speaking, and with the kind of voice you'd be apt to notice . . . yes, I see she's the girl you've been looking for. I can give you the New York people's address, but first, for Jane's sake, — I'm a pretty good friend of hers, I think a lot of Jane, — I'll have to know what you want with her — what she is to you."

Pierre's pupils widened till they all but swallowed the smoke-colored iris.

"She is my wife," he said.

Again Yarnall swore. But he lit a cigarette and took his time about answering. "Well, sir," he said, "you must excuse me, but — it was because she saw you, I take it, that Jane cut off this morning. That's clear. Now, I don't know what would make a girl run off from her husband. She might have any number of reasons, bad and good, but it seems to me that it would be a pretty strong one that would make a girl run off, with a look such as she wore, from a man like you. Did you treat her well, Landis?"

It had the effect of a lash taken by a penitent. The man shrank a little, whitened, endured. "I can't tell you how I treated her," he said in a dangerous voice; "it don't bear tellin'. But — I want her back. I was — I was — that was three years ago; I am more like a man now. You'll give me the people's name, their address? . . ."

Pierre laid his hand on the older man's wrist and gave it a queer urgent and beseeching shake.

After a moment of searching scrutiny, Yarnall bent his head.

"Very well," said he shortly; "come in."

CHAPTER V

LUCK'S PLAY

A YOUNG man who had just landed in New York from one of the big, adventurous transatlantic liners hailed a taxicab and was quickly drawn away into the glitter and gayety of a bright winter morning. He sat forward eagerly, looking at everything with the air of a lad on a holiday. He was a young man, but he was not in his first youth, and under a heavy sunburn he was pale and a trifle worn, but there was about him a look of being hard and very much alive. Under a broad brow there were hawk eyes of greenish gray, a delicate beak, a mouth and chin of cleverness. It was an interesting face and looked as though it had seen interesting things. In fact, Prosper Gael had just returned from his three months of ambulance service in France, and it was the extraordinary success of his play, "The Leopardess," that had chiefly brought him back.

"Dear Luck," his manager had written, using the college title which Prosper's name and unvarying good fortune suggested, "you'd better come back and gather up some of these laurels that are smothering us all. The time is very favorable for the disappearance of your anonymity. I, for one, find it more and more difficult to keep the secret. So far, not even your star knows it. She calls you 'Mr. Luck' . . . to that extent I have been indiscreet. . . ."

Prosper had another letter in his pocket, a letter that he had re-read many times, always with an uneasy conflict of emotions. He was in a sort of hot-cold humor over it, in a fever-fit that had a way of turning into lassitude. He postponed analysis indefinitely. Meanwhile his eyes searched the bright, cold city, its crowds, its traffics, its windows — most of all, its placards, and, not far to seek, there were the posters of "The Leopardess." He leaned out to study one of them; a tall, wild-eyed woman crouched to spring upon a man who stared at her in fear. Prosper dropped back with a gleaming smile of amused excitement. "They've made it look like cheap melodrama," he said to himself; "and yet it's a good thing, the best thing I've ever done. Yet they will vulgarize the whole idea with their infernal notions of 'what the public wants.' Morena is as bad as the rest of them!" He expressed disgust, but underneath he was aglow with pride and interest. "There's a performance to-night. I'll dine with Jasper. I'll have to see Betty first . . ." His thoughts trailed off and he fell into that hot-cold confusion, that uncomfortable scorching fog of mood. The cab turned into Fifth Avenue and became a scale in the creeping serpent of vehicles that glided, paused, and glided again past the thronged pavements. Prosper contrasted everything with the grim courage and high-pitched tragedy of France. He could not but wonder at the detached frivolity of these money-spenders, these spinners in the sun. How soon would the shadow fall upon them too and with what change of countenance would they look up! To him the joyousness seemed almost childish and yet he bathed his fagged spirit in it. How high the white clouds sailed, how blue was the midwinter sky! How the buildings towered, how quickly the people stepped! Here were the pretty painted faces, the absurd silk stockings, the tripping, exquisitely booted feet, the swinging walk, the tall, upspringing bodies of the women he remembered. He regarded them with impersonal delight, untinged by any of his usual cynicism.

It was late afternoon when Prosper, obedient to a telephone call from Betty, presented himself at the door of Morena's house, just east of the Park, off Fifth Avenue; a very beautiful house where the wealthy Jew had indulged his passion for exquisite things. Prosper entered its rich dimness with a feeling of oppression — that unanalyzed mood of hot and cold feeling intensified to an almost unbearable degree. In the large carved and curtained drawing-room he waited for Betty. The tea-things were prepared; there would be no further need of service until Betty should ring. Everything was arranged for an uninterrupted tête-à-tête. Prosper stood near an ebony table, his shoulder brushed by tall, red roses, and felt his nerves tighten and his pulses hasten in their beat. "The tall child . . . the tall child . . ." he had called her by that name so often and never without a swift and stabbing memory of Joan, and of Joan's laughter which he had silenced.

He took out the letter he had lately received from Betty and re-read it and, as he read, a deep line cut between his eyes. "You say you will not come back unless I can give you more than I have ever given you in the past. You say you intend to cut yourself free, that I have failed you too often, that you are starved on hope. I'm not going to ask much more patience of you. I failed you that first time because I lost courage; the second time, fate failed us. How could I think that Jasper would get well when the doctors told me that I must n't allow myself even a shadow of hope! Now, I think that Jasper, himself, is preparing my release. This all sounds like something in a book. That's because you've hurt me. I feel frozen up. I could n't bear it if now, just when the door is opening, you failed me. Prosper, you are my lover for always, are n't you? I have to believe that to go on living. You are the one thing in my wretched life that has n't lost its value. Now, read this carefully; I am going to be brutal. Jasper has been unfaithful to me. I know it. I have sufficient evidence to prove it in a law court and I shall not hesitate to get a divorce. Tear this up, please. Now, of all times, we must be extraordinarily careful. There has never been a whisper against us and there must n't be. Jasper must not suspect. A counter-suit would ruin my life. I must talk it over with you. I'll see you once alone — just once — before I leave Jasper and begin the suit. We must have patience for just this last bit. It will seem very long . . ."

Prosper folded the letter. He was conscious of a faint feeling of sickness, of fear. Then he heard Betty's step across the marble pavement of the hall. She parted the heavy curtains, drew them together behind her, and stood, pale with joy, opening and shutting her big eyes. Then she came to meet him, held him back, listening for any sound that might predict interruption, and gave herself to his arms. She was no longer pale when he let her go. She went a few steps away and stood with her hands before her face, then she went to sit by the tea-table. They were both flushed. Betty's eyes were shining under their fluttering lids. Prosper rejoiced in his own emotion. The mental fog had lifted and the feeling of faintness was gone.

"You 've decided not to break away altogether, then?" she asked, giving him a quick glance.

He shook his head. "Not if what you have written me is true. I've had such letters from you before and I 've grown very suspicious. Are you sure this time?" He laid stress upon his bitterness. It was his one weapon against her and he had been sharpening it with a vague purpose.

"Oh," said Betty, speaking low and furtively, "Jasper is fairly caught. I have a reliable witness in the girl's maid. There is no doubt of his guilt, Prosper, none. Everyone is talking of it. He has been perfectly open in his attentions."

Every minute Betty looked younger and prettier, more provoking. Her child-mouth with its clever smile was bright as though his kiss had painted it.

"Who is the girl?" asked Prosper. He was deeply flushed. Being capable of simultaneous points of view, he had been stung by that cool phrase of Betty's concerning "Jasper's guilt."

"I'll tell you in a moment. Did you destroy my letter?"

He shook his head.

"Oh, Prosper, please!"

He took it out, tore it up, and walking over to the open fire, burned the papers. He came back to his tea. "Well, Betty?"

"The girl," said Betty, "is the star in your play, 'The Leopardess,' the girl that Jasper picked up two Septembers ago out West. He has written to you about her. She was a cook, if you please, a hideous creature, but Jasper saw at once what there was in her. She has made the play. You'll have to acknowledge that yourself when you see her. She is wonderful. And, partly owing to the trouble I've taken with her, the girl is beautiful. One would n't have thought it possible. She is not charming to me, she's not in the least subtle. It's odd that she should have had such an effect upon Jasper, of all men . . ."

Prosper sipped his tea and listened. He looked

at her and was bitterly conscious that the excitement which had pleased and surprised him was dying out. That faintness again assailed his spirit. He was feeling stifled, ashamed, bored. Yes, that was it, bored. That life of service and battle-danger in France had changed him more than he had realized till now. He was more simple, more serious, more moral, in a certain sense. He was like a man who, having denied the existence of Apollyon, has come upon him face to face and has been burnt by his breath. Such a man is inevitably moral. All this long, intricate intrigue with the wife of a man who called him friend, seemed to him horribly unworthy. If Betty had been a great lover, if she had not lost courage at the eleventh hour and left him to face that terrible winter in Wyoming, then their passion might have justified itself: but now there was a staleness in their relationship. He hated the thought of the long divorce proceedings, of the decent interval, of the wedding, of the married life. He had never really wanted that. And now, in the ebb of his passion, how could he force himself to take her when he had learned to live more keenly, more completely without her! He would have to take her, to spend his days and nights with her, to travel with her. She would want to visit that gay, little forsaken house in a Wyoming cañon. With vividness he saw a girl lying prone on a black rug before a dancing fire, her hair all fallen about her face, her secret eyes lifted impatiently from the book — "You had ought to be writin', Mr. Gael . . ."

"What are you smiling for, Prosper?" Betty asked sharply.

He looked up, startled and confused. "Sorry. I've got into beastly absent-minded habits. Is that Morena?"

Jasper opened the curtains and came in, greeting Prosper in his stately, charming fashion. "To-night," he said, "we'll show you a leopardess worth looking at, won't we, Betty? But first you must tell us about your own experience. You look wonderfully fit, does n't he, Betty? And changed. They say the life out there stamps a man, and they're right. It's taken some of that winged-demon look out of your face, Prosper, put some soul into it."

He talked and Betty laughed, showing not the slightest evidence of effort, though the soul Jasper had seen in Prosper's face felt shriveled for her treachery. Prosper wondered if she could be right in her surmise about Jasper. The Jew was infinitely capable of dissimulation, but there was a clarity of look and smile that filled Prosper with doubts. And the eyes he turned upon his wife were quite as apparently as ever the eyes of a disappointed man.

So absorbed was he in such observations that he found it intolerably difficult to fix his attention on the talk. Jasper's fluency seemed to ripple senselessly about his brain.

"You must consent to one thing, Luck: you must allow me to choose my own time for announcing the authorship." This found its way partially to his intelligence and he gave careless assent.

"Oh, whenever you like, as soon as I've had my fun."

"Of course —" Morena was thoughtful for an instant. "How would it do for me to leave it with Melton, the business manager? Eh? Suppose I phone him and talk it over a little. He'll want to wait till toward the end of the run. He's keen; has just the commercial sense of the born advertiser. Let him choose the moment. Then we can feel sure of getting the right one. Will you, Luck?"

"If you advise it. You ought to know."

"You see, I'm so confoundedly busy, so many irons in the fire, I might just miss the psychic moment. I think Melton's the man — I'll call him up to-night before we leave. Then I won't forget it and I'll be sure to catch him too."

Again Prosper vaguely agreed and promptly forgot that he had given his permission. Later, there came an agonizing moment when he would have given the world to recall his absent, careless words.

With an effort Prosper kept his poise, with an effort, always increasing, he talked to Jasper while Betty dressed, and kept up his end at dinner. The muscles round his mouth felt tight and drawn, his throat was dry. He was glad when they got into the limousine and started theaterwards. It had been a long time since he had been put through this particular ordeal and he was out of practice.

They reached the house just as the lights went out. Prosper was amused at his own intense excitement. "I did n't know I was still such a kid," he said, flashing a smile, the first spontaneous one he had given her, upon Betty who sat beside him in the proscenium box.

The success of his novel had had no such effect upon him as this. It was entrancing to think that in a few moments the words he had written would come to him clothed in various voices, the people his brain had pictured would move before him in flesh and blood, doing what he had ordained that they should do. When the curtain rose, he had forgotten his personal problem, had forgotten Betty. He leaned forward, his elbows on his knees, his chin in his hand.

The scene was of a tropical island, palms, a strip of turquoise sea. A girl pushed aside the great fronds of ferns and stepped down to the beach. At her appearance the audience broke into applause. She was a tall girl, her stained legs and arms bare below her ragged dress, her black hair hung wild and free about her face and neck. As the daughter of a native mother and an English father, her beauty had been made to seem both Saxon and savage. Stained and painted, darkened below the great gray eyes, Joan with her brows and her classic chin and throat, Joan with her secret, dangerous eyes and lithe, long body, made an arresting picture enough against the setting of vivid green and blue. She moved slowly, deliberately, naturally, and stood, hands on hips, to watch a ship sail into the turquoise harbor. It was not like acting, she seemed really to look. She threw back her head and gave a call. It was the name of her stage brother, but it came from her deep chest and through her long column of a throat like music. Prosper brought down his hands on the railing before him, half pushed himself up, turned a blind look upon Betty, who laid a restraining hand upon his arm.

He whispered a name, which Betty could not make out, then he sat down, moistened his lips with his tongue, and sat through the entire first act and neither moved nor spoke. As the curtain went down he stood up.

"I must go out," he said, and hesitated in the back of the box till Jasper came over to him with an anxious question. Then he began to stammer nervously. "Don't tell her, Jasper, don't tell her."

"Tell her what, man? Tell whom?" Jasper gave him a shake. "Don't you like Jane? Is n't she wonderful?"

"Yes, yes, extraordinary!"

"Made for the part?"

"No." Prosper's face twisted into a smile. "No. The part came second, she was there first. Morena, promise me you won't tell her who wrote the play."

"Look here, Prosper, suppose you tell me what's wrong. Have you seen a ghost?"

Prosper laughed; then, seeing Betty, her face a rigid question, he struggled to lay hands upon his self-control.

"Something very astonishing has happened, Morena, — one of those 'things not dreamt of in a man's philosophy.' I can't tell you. Have you arranged for me to meet Jane West?"

"After the show, yes, at supper."

"But not as the author?"

"No. I was waiting for you to tell her that."

"She must n't know. And — and I can't meet her that way, at supper." Again he made visible efforts at self-control. "Don't tell Betty what a fool I am. I'll go out a minute. I'll be all right."

Betty was coming toward them. He gave a painful smile and fled.

CHAPTER VI

JOAN AND PROSPER

THE situation was no doubt an extraordinary, an unimaginable one, but it had to be met. When he returned to the box, Prosper had himself in hand, and, sitting a little farther back than before, he watched the second act with a sufficiency of outward calm.

This part was the most severe test of his composure, for he had fashioned it almost in detail upon that idyll in a cañon. There were even speeches of Joan's that he had used. To sit here and watch Joan herself go through it, while he looked on, was an exciting form of torment. The setting was different, tropical instead of Northern, and the half-native heroine was more passionate, more emotional, more animal than Joan. Nevertheless, the drama was a repetition. As Prosper had laid his trap for Joan, silently, subtly undermining her whole mental structure, using her loneliness, playing upon the artist soul of her, so did this Englishman lay his trap for Zona. He was more cruel than Prosper, rougher, necessarily more dramatic, but there was all the essence of the original drama, the ensnarement of a simple, direct mind by a complex and skillful one. Joan's surrender, Prosper's victory, were there. He wondered how Joan could act it, play the part in cold blood. Now he was condemned to live in his own imagination through Joan's tragedy. There was that first pitifulness of a tamed and broken spirit; then later, in London, the agony of loneliness, of separation, of gradual awakening to the change in her master's heart. Prosper had written the words, but it was Joan who, with her voice, the music of memory-shaken heart-strings, made the words alive and meaningful. Others in the audience might wonder over the girl's ability to interpret this unusual experience, to make it natural, human, inevitable. But Prosper did not wonder. He knew that simply she forced herself to re-live this most painful part of her own life and to re-live it articulately. What, in God's name, had induced her to do it? Necessity? Poverty? Morena? All at once he remembered Betty's belief, that Joan was the manager's mistress — his wild, beautiful Joan, Joan the creation of his own wizardry. This thought gave him such pain that he whitened.

"Prosper," murmured Betty, "you must tell me what is wrong. Evidently your nerves are in bad shape. Is the excitement too much for you?"

"I believe it is," he said, avoiding her eyes and moving stiff, white lips; "I've never seen such acting. I — I— Morena says he'll let me see her in her dressing-room afterwards. You see, Betty, I'm badly shaken up."

"Ye-es," drawled Betty, and looked at him through narrowed lids, and she sat with this look on her face and with her fingers locked, when Prosper, not giving her further notice, followed Morena out.

"Jasper," — Prosper held his friend back in the middle of a passage that led to the dressing-rooms, — "I want very particularly to see Miss West alone. I am very much moved by her performance and I want to tell her so. Also, I want her to express herself naturally with no idea of my being the author of the play and without the presence of her manager. Will you just ask if she will see a friend of yours — alone?"

Jasper smiled his subtle smile. "Of course, Prosper. It's all as clear as daylight."

Prosper did not notice the Jew's intelligent expression. He was too much absorbed in his own excitement. In a moment he would be with Joan — Joan, his love of winter nights!

Morena tapped upon a door. A maid half-opened it.

"Ask Miss West, please, if she will see a friend of Mr. Morena's. Tell her I particularly wish her to give him a private interview." He scribbled a line on a card and the maid took it in.

In five minutes, during which the two men waited silently, she came back.

"Miss West will see your friend, sir."

"Ah! Then I'll take myself off. Prosper, will you join Betty and me at supper?"

"No, thanks. I'll have my brief interview with Miss West and then go home, if you'll forgive me. I'm about all in. New York's too much for a man just home from the front."

Jasper laid his hand for a moment on Prosper's shoulder, smiled, shrugged, and turned away. Prosper waited till his friend was out of sight and hearing, then knocked and was admitted to the dressing-room of Miss Jane West.

She had not changed from the evening dress she had worn in the last scene nor had she yet got rid of her make-up. She was sitting in a narrow-backed chair that had been turned away from the dressing-table. The maid was putting away some costumes.

Prosper walked half across the room and stopped.

"Miss West," he said quietly.

She stood up. The natural color left her face ghastly with patches of paint and daubs of black. She threw back her head and said, "Prosper!" just above her breath.

"Go out, Henrietta." This was spoken to the maid in the voice of Jane the virago and Henrietta fled.

At sight of Joan, Prosper had won back instantly his old poise, his old feeling of ascendancy.

"Joan, Joan," he said gently; "was ever anything so strange? Why did n't you let me know? Why did n't you answer my letters? Why did n't you take my money? I have suffered greatly on your account."

Joan laughed. Four years ago she would not have been capable of this laugh, and Prosper started.

"I wrote again and again," he said passionately. "Wen Ho told me that you had gone, that he did n't know anything about your plans. I went out to Wyoming, to our house. I scoured the country for you. Did you know that?"

"No," said Joan slowly, "I did n't know that. But it makes no difference to me."

They were still standing a few paces apart, too intent upon their inner tumult to heed any outward situation. She lowered her head in that dangerous way of hers, looking up at him from under her brows. Her color had returned and the make-up had a more natural look.

"Maybe you did write, maybe you did send money, maybe you did come back — I don't care anything for all that." She made a gesture as if to sweep something away. "The day after you left me in that house, Pierre, my husband, came up the trail. He was taking after me. He meant to fetch me home. You told me" — she began to tremble so violently that the jewels on her neck clicked softly — "you told me he was *dead.*"

Prosper came closer, she moving back, till, striking the chair, she sat down on it and looked up at him with her changed and embittered eyes.

"Would you have gone back to him, Joan Landis, after he had tied you up and branded your shoulder with his cattlebrand?"

"What has that got to do with it?" she asked, her voice lifting on a wave of anger. "That was between my man and me. That was not for you to judge. He loved me. It was through loving me too much, too ignorantly, that he hurt me so." She choked. "But you —"

"Joan," said Prosper, and he laid his hand on her cold and rigid fingers, "I loved you too."

She was still and stiff. After a long silence she seemed to select one question from a tide of them.

"Why did you leave me?"

"I wrote you a full explanation. The letter came back to me unread."

Again Joan gave the laugh and the gesture of disdain.

"That does n't matter . . . your loving or not loving. You made use of me for your own ends, and when you saw fit, you left me. But that's not my complaint. I don't say I did n't deserve that. I was easy to use. But it was all based on what was n't true. I was married, my man was living, and I had dealings with you. That was sin. That was horrible. That was what my mother did. She was a ——" Joan used the coarse and ugly word her father had taught her, and Prosper laid a hand over her mouth.

"Joan! No! Never say it, never think it. You are clean."

Joan twisted herself free, stood up, and walked away. "I am *that!*" she said grimly; "and it was you that made me. You took lots of trouble to make me see things in a way where nothing a person wants is either right or wrong. You made me thirsty with your talk and your books and your music, and when I was tormented with thirst, you came and offered me a drink of water. That was it. I don't care about your not marrying me. I still don't see that that has much to do with it except, perhaps, that a man would be caring to give any woman he rightly loves whatever help or cherishing or gifts the world has decided to give her. But, you see, Prosper, we did n't start fair. You knew that Pierre was alive."

"But, Joan, you say yourself that marrying—"

She stopped him with so fierce a gesture that he flinched. "Yes. Pierre did rightly love me. He gave me his best as he knew it. Oh, he was ignorant, a savage, I guess, like I was. But he did rightly love me. He was not trying to break my spirit nor to tame me, nor to amuse himself with me, nor to give me a longing for beauty and easiness and then leave me to fight through my own rough life without any of those things. Did you really think, Prosper Gael, that I would stay in your house and live on your money till you should be caring to come back to me — if ever you would care? Did you honestly think that you would be coming back — as — as my lover? No. Whatever it was that took you away, it was likely to keep you from me for always, was n't it?"

"Yes," said Prosper in a muffled voice, "it was likely to. But, Joan, Fate was on your side. Since I have been yours, I have n't belonged to any one but you. You've put your brand on me."

"I don't want to hear about you," Joan broke in. "I am done with you. Have you seen this play?"

"Yes." He found that in telling her so he could not meet her eyes.

"Well, the man who wrote that knew what you are, and, if he did n't, every one that has seen me act in it, knows what you are." She paused, breathing fast and trembling. "Good-bye," she said.

He went vaguely toward the door, then threw up his head defiantly. "No," he said, "it's not going to be good-bye. I've found you. You must let me tell you the truth about myself. Come, Joan, you're as just as Heaven. You never read my explanations. You've never heard my side of it. You'll let me come to see you and you'll hear me out. Don't do me an injustice. I'll leave the whole thing in your hands after that. But you must give me that one chance."

"Chance?" repeated Joan. "Chance for what?"

"Oh," — Prosper flung up his lithe, long hands — "oh, for nothing but a cleansing in your sight. I want what forgiveness I can wring from you. I want what understanding I can force from you. That's all."

She thought, standing there, still and tall, her arms hanging, her eyes wide and secret, as he had remembered them in her thin, changed, so much more expressive face.

"Very well," she said, "you may come. I'll hear you out." She gave him the address and named an afternoon hour. "Good-night."

It was a graceful and dignified dismissal. Prosper bit his lip, bowed and left her.

As the door closed upon her, he knew that it had closed upon the only real and vivid presence in his life. War had burnt away his glittering, clever frivolity. Betty was the adventure, Betty was the tinsel; Joan was the grave, predestined woman of his man. For the first time in his life he found himself face to face with the cleanness of despair.

CHAPTER VII

AFTERMATH

JOAN waited for Prosper on the appointed afternoon. There was a fire on her hearth and a March snow-squall tapped against the window panes. The crackle of the logs inside and that eerie, light sound outside were so associated with Prosper that, even before he came, Joan, sitting on one side of the hearth, closed her eyes and felt that he must be opposite to her in his red-lacquered chair, his long legs stuck out in front, his amused and greedy eyes veiled by a cloud of cigarette smoke.

Since she had seen him at the theater, she had been suffering from sleeplessness. At night she would go over and over the details of their intercourse, seeing them, feeling them, living them in the light of later knowledge, till the torment was hardly to be borne. Three days and nights of this inner activity had brought back that sharp line between her brows and the bitter tightening of her lips.

This afternoon she was white with suspense. Her dread of the impending interview was like a physical illness. She sat in a high-backed chair, hands along the arms, head resting back, eyes half-closed, in that perfect stillness of which the animal and the savage are alone entirely capable. There were many gifts that Joan had brought from the seventeen years on Lone River. This grave immobility was one. She was very carefully dressed in a gown that accentuated her height and dignity. And she wore a few jewels. She wanted, pitifully enough, to mark every difference between this Joan and the Joan whom Prosper had drawn on his sled up the cañon trail. If he expected to force her back into the position of enchanted leopardess, to see her "lie at his feet and eat out of his hand," as Morena had once described the plight of Zona, he would see at a glance that she was no longer so easily mastered. In fact, sitting there, she looked as proud and perilous as a young Medea, black-haired with long throat and cold, malevolent lips. It was only in the eyes — those gray, unhappy, haunted eyes — that Joan gave away her eternal simplicity of heart. They were unalterably tender and lonely and hurt. It was the look in them that had prompted Shorty's description, "She's plumb movin' to me — looks about halfway between 'You go to hell' and 'You take me in your arms to rest.'"

Prosper was announced, and Joan, keeping her stillness, merely turned her head toward him as he came into the room.

She saw his rapid observation of the room, of her, even before she noticed the very apparent change in him. For he, too, was haggard and utterly serious as she did not remember him. He stood before her fire and asked her jerkily if she would let him smoke. She said "Yes," and those were the only words spoken for five unbearable minutes the seconds of which her heart beat out like a shaky hammer in some worn machine.

Prosper smoked and stood there looking, now at her, now at the fire. At last, with difficulty, he smiled. "You are not going to make it easy for me, are you, Joan?"

For her part she was not looking at him. She kept her eyes on the fire and this averted look distressed and irritated his nerves.

"I am not trying to make it hard," she said; "I want you to say what you came to say and go."

"Did *you* ever love me, Joan?"

He had said it to force a look from her, but it had the effect only of making her more still, if possible.

"I don't know," she said slowly, answering

with her old directness. "I thought you needed me. I was alone. I was scared of the emptiness when I went out and looked down the valley. I thought Pierre had gone out of the world and there was no living thing that wanted me. I came back and you met me and you put your arms round me and you said" — she closed her eyes and repeated his speech as though she had just heard it — "'Don't leave me, Joan.'"

Her voice was more than ever before moving and expressive. Prosper felt that half-forgotten thrill. The muscles of his throat contracted. "Joan, I did want you. I spoke the truth," he pleaded.

She went on with no impatience but very coldly. "You came to tell me your side. Will you tell me, please?"

For the first time she looked into his eyes and he drew in his breath at the misery of hers.

"I built that cabin, Joan," he said, "for another woman."

"Your wife?" asked Joan.

"No."

"For the one I said must have been like a tall child? She was n't your wife? She was dead?"

Prosper shook his head. "No. Did you think that? She was a woman I loved at that time very dearly and she was already married to another man."

"You built that house for her? I don't understand."

"She had promised to leave her husband and to come away with me. I had everything ready, those rooms, those clothes, those materials, and when I went out to get her, I had a message saying that her courage had failed her, that she would n't come."

"She was a better woman than me," said Joan bitterly.

Prosper laughed. "By God, she was not! She sent me down to hell. I could n't go back to the East again. I had laid very careful and elaborate plans. I was trapped out there in that horrible winter country . . ."

"It was not horrible," said Joan violently; "it was the most wonderful, beautiful country in all the world." And tears ran suddenly down her face.

But she would not let him come near to comfort her. "Go on," she said presently.

"Before you came, Joan," Prosper went on, "it was horrible. It was like being starved. Every thing in the house reminded me of — her. I had planned it all very carefully and we were to have been — happy. You can fancy what it was to be there alone."

Joan nodded. She *was* just and she was honestly trying to put herself in his place. "Yes," she said; "if I had gone back and Pierre had been dead, his homestead would have been like that to me."

"It was because I was so miserable that I went out to hunt. I'd scour the country all day and half the night to tire myself out, that I could get some sleep. I was pretty far from home that moonlight night when I heard you scream for help . . ."

Joan's face grew whiter. "Don't tell about that," she pleaded.

He paused, choosing another opening. "After I had bandaged you and told you that Pierre was dead — and I honestly thought he was — I did n't know what to do with you. You could n't be left, and there was no neighbor nearer than my own house; besides, I had shot a man, and, perhaps, — I don't know, maybe I was influenced by your beauty, by my own crazy loneliness. . . . You were very beautiful and very desolate. I was in a fury over the brute's treatment of you . . ."

"Hush!" said Joan; "you are not to talk about Pierre."

Prosper shrugged. "I decided to take you home with me. I wanted you desperately, just, I believe, to take care of, just to be kind to — truly, Joan, I was lonely to the point of madness. Some one to care for, some one to talk to, was absolutely necessary to save my reason. So when I was leading you out, I — I saw Pierre's hand move —"

Joan stood up. After a moment she controlled herself with an effort and sat down again. "Go on. I can stand it," she said.

"And I thought to myself, 'The devil is alive and he deserves to be dead. This woman can never live with him again. God would n't sanction such an act as giving her back to his hands.' And I was half-mad myself, I'd been alone so long . . . I stood so you could n't see him, Joan, and I threw an elk-hide over him and led you out."

"I followed you; I did n't look at Pierre; I left him lying there," gasped Joan.

Prosper went on monotonously. "When I came back a week later, I thought he would be dead. It was dusk, the wind was blowing, the snow was driving in a scud. I came down to the cabin and dropped below the drift by that northern window, and, the second I looked in, I dropped out of sight. There was a light and a fire. Your husband was lying before the fire on a cot. There was another man there, your Mr. Holliwell; they were talking, Holliwell was dressing Pierre's wound. I went away like a ghost, and while I was going back, I thought it all out; and I decided to keep you for myself. I suppose," said Prosper dully, "that that was a horrible sin. I did n't see it that way then. I'm not sure I see it that way now. Pierre had tied you up and pressed a white-hot iron into your bare shoulder. If you went back to him, if he took you back, how was I to know that he might not repeat his drunken deviltry, or do worse, if anything could be worse! It was the act of a fiend. It put him out of court with me. Whatever I gave you, education and beauty, and ease, must be better and happier for you than life with such a brute as Pierre —"

"Stop!" said Joan between her teeth; "you know nothing of Pierre and me; you only know that one dreadful night. You don't know — the rest."

"I don't want to know the rest," he said sharply; "that is enough to justify my action. I thought so then and I think so now. You won't be able to make me change that opinion."

"I shall not try," said Joan.

He accepted this and went on. "When I found you in your bed waiting for news of Pierre, I thought you the most beautiful, pitiful thing I had ever seen. I loved you then, Joan, then. Tell me, did I ever in those days hurt you or give you a moment's anxiety or fear?"

"No," Joan admitted, "you did not. In those days you were wonderful, kind and patient with me. I thought you were more like God than a human then."

Prosper laughed with bitterness. "You thought very wrong, but, according to my own lights, I was very careful of you. I meant to give you all I could and I meant to win you with patience and forbearance. I had respect for you and for your grief and for the horrible thing you had suffered. Joan, by now you know better what the world is. Can you reproach me so very bitterly for our — happiness, even if it was short?"

"You lied to me," said Joan. "It was n't just. We did n't start even. And — and you knew what you wanted of me. I never guessed."

"You did n't? You never guessed?"

"No. Sometimes, toward the last, I was afraid. I felt that I ought to go away. That day I ran off — you remember — I was afraid of you. I felt you were bad and that I was bad too. Then it seemed to me that I'd been dreadfully ungrateful and unkind. That was what began to make me give way to my feelings. I was sorrowful because I had hurt you and you so kind! The day I came in with that suit and spoke of — her as a 'tall child' and you cried, why, I felt so sorrowful that I'd made you suffer. I wanted to comfort you, to put my hands on you in comfort, like a mother, I felt. And you went out like you were angry and stayed away all night as though you could n't bear to be seeing me again in your house that you had built for her. So I wrote you my letter and went away. And then — it was all so awful cold and empty. I did n't know Pierre was out there. I came back . . ."

They were both silent for a long time and in the silence the idyll was re-lived. Spring came again with its crest of green along the cañon and the lake lay like a turquoise drawing the glittering peak down into its heart.

"My book — its success," Prosper began at last, "made me restless. You'll understand that now that you are an artist yourself. And one day there came a letter from that woman I had loved."

"It was a little square gray envelope," said

Joan breathlessly. "I can see it now. You never rightly looked at me again."

"Ah!" said Prosper. He turned and hid his face.

"Tell me the rest," said Joan.

He went on without turning back to her, his head bent. "The woman wrote that her husband was dying, that I must come back to her at once."

The snow tapped and the fire crackled.

"And when you — went back?"

"Her husband did not die," said Prosper blankly; "he is still alive."

"And you still love her very much?"

"That's the worst of it, Joan," groaned Prosper. His groan changed into a desperate laugh. "I love you. Now truly I do love you. If I could marry you — if I could have you for my wife —" He waited, breathing fast, then came and stood close before her. "I have never wanted a woman to be my wife till now. I want you. I want you to be the mother of my children."

Then Joan did look at him with all her eyes.

"I am Pierre's wife," she said. The liquid beauty had left her voice. It was hoarse and dry. "I am Pierre's wife and I have already been the mother of your child."

There was a long, rigid silence. "Joan — when? — where?" Prosper's throat clicked.

"I knew it before you left. I could n't tell you because you were so changed. I worked all winter. It — it was born on an awful cold March night. I think the woman let it — made it — die. She wanted me to work for her during the summer and she thought I would be glad if the child did n't live. She used to say I was 'in trouble' and she'd be glad if she could 'help me out.' . . . It was what I was planning to live for . . . that child."

During the heavy stillness following Joan's dreadful, brief account of birth and death, Prosper went through a strange experience. It seemed to him that in his soul something was born and died. Always afterwards there was a ghost in him — the father that might have been.

"I can't talk any more," said Joan faintly. "Won't you please go?"

CHAPTER VIII

AGAINST THE BARS

JASPER MORENA had stood for an hour in a drafty passage of that dirty labyrinth known vaguely to the public as "behind the scenes," listening to the wearisome complaints of a long-nosed young actor. It was the sixth of such conversations that he had held that day: to begin with, there had been a difficulty between a director and the leading man. Morena's tact was still complete; he was very gentle to the long-nosed youth; but the latter, had he been capable of seeing anything but himself, must have noticed that his listener's face was pale and faintly lined.

"Yes, my boy, of course, that's reasonable enough. I'll do what I can."

"I don't make extravagant demands, you see," the young man spread down and out his hands, quivering with exaggerated feeling; "I ask only for decent treatment, what my own self-respect ab-so-lute-ly demands."

Morena put a hand on his shoulder and walked beside him.

"Did you ever stop to think," he said with his charming smile, "that the other fellow is thinking and saying just the same thing? Now, this chap that has, as you put it, got your goat, why, he came to me himself this morning, and, word for word, he said of you just precisely what you have just said of him to me. Odd, is n't it?"

Again the young actor stopped for one of his gestures, hands up this time. "But, my God, sir! Is there such a thing as honesty? He could n't accuse me of —"

"Well, he thought he could. However, I do get your point of view and I think we can fix it up for you so that you'll get off with your self-respect entirely intact. I'll talk to George to-morrow. You're worth the bother. Good-afternoon."

The young man bowed, his air of tragic injury softened to one of tragic self-appreciation. Worth the bother, indeed!

Morena left him at the top of the dingy stairs down which the manager fled to an alley at one side of the theater, where his car was waiting for him. He stood for a while with his foot on the step and his hand on the door, looking rather blankly at the gray, cold wall and the scurrying whirlwinds of dust and paper.

"Drop yourself at the garage, Ned," he said, "and I'll take the car."

He climbed in beside the wheel. He was very tired, but he had remembered that Jane West, when he had last seen her, had worn a look of profound discouragement. She never complained, but when he saw that particular expression he was frightened and the responsibility for her came heavily upon him. This wild thing he had brought to New York must not be allowed to beat its head dumbly against the bars.

When he had got rid of his driver, he turned the car northward, and a few minutes later Mathilde, the French maid chosen by Betty, opened Jane's door to him.

While he took off his coat he looked along the hall and saw its owner sitting, her chin propped on a latticework of fingers. She was gazing out of the window. It was a beautiful, desperate silhouette; something fateful in the long, still pose and the fixed look. She was still dressed in street clothes as when she had left the theater, a blouse and skirt of dark gray, very plain. Her figure, now that it was trained to slight corseting, was less vigorous and more fine-drawn. She was very thin, but she had lost her worn and haggard look; the premature hard lines had almost disappeared;

a softer climate, proper care, rest, food, luxury had given back her young, clear skin and the brightness of eyes and lips. Her hair, arranged very simply to frame her face in a broken setting of black, was glossy, and here and there, deeply waved. It was the arrangement chosen for her by Betty and copied from a Du Maurier drawing of the Duchess of Towers. It was hard to believe that this graceful woman was the virago Jane, harder for any one that had seen a heavy, handsome girl stride into Mrs. Upper's hotel and ask for work, to believe that she was here.

Morena clapped his hands in the Eastern fashion of summons, and Jane looked toward him.

"Oh," she said, "I'm glad you came."

He strolled in and stood beside her shaking his head.

"I did n't like the look of you this afternoon, my dear."

"Well, sir," said Jane, "I don't like the look of you either." She smiled her slow, unselfconscious smile. "You sit down and I'll make tea for you."

He knew that thought for some one else was the best tonic for her mood, so he dropped, with his usual limp grace, into the nearest chair, put back his head and half-closed his eyes.

"I'm used up," he said; "I have n't a word — not one to throw at a dog."

"Please don't throw one at me, then. I surely would n't take it as a compliment." She made the tea gravely, as absorbed in the work as a little girl who makes tea for her dolls. She brought him his cup and went back to her place and again her face settled into that look. She had evidently forgotten him and her eyes held a vision as of distances.

He put a hand up to break her fixed gaze. "What is it, Jane? What do you see?"

To his astonishment she hid her face in her hands. "It's awful to live like this," she moaned; and it frightened him to see her move her head from side to side like an imprisoned beast, shifting before bars.

He looked about the pretty room and repeated, "Like this?" half-reproachfully.

"I hate it!" She spoke through her teeth. "I hate it! And, oh, the sounds, the noises, grinding into your ears."

Here the hands came to her ears and framed a white, desperate face in which the lids had fallen over sick eyes.

Jasper sat listening to the hum and roar and clatter of the street. To him it was a pleasant sound, and here it was subdued and remote enough. Her face was like that of some one maddened by noise.

"You don't smell anything fresh" — her chest lifted — "you don't get air. I can't breathe. Everything presses in." She opened her eyes, bright and desperate. "What am I doing here, Mr. Morena?"

He had put down his cup quietly, for he was really half-afraid of her. "Why did you come, Jane?"

"Because I was afraid of some one. I was running away, Mr. Morena. There's some one that must n't ever find me now, and to run away from him — that was the business of my life. And it kept my heart full of him and the dread of his coming. You see, that was my happiness. I hoped he was taking after me so's I could run away." She laughed apologetically. "Does that sound crazy to you?"

"No. I think I understand. And here?"

"He'll never come here. He'll never find me. It's been four years. And I'm so changed. This" — she gave herself a downward look — "this is n't the 'gel' he wants. . . . Probably by now he's given me up. Maybe he's found another. Everything that's bad and hateful can find me out here. Bad things can find you out and try to clutch after you anywheres. But when something wild and clean comes hunting for you, something out of the big lonely places — why, it would be scared to follow into this city."

"You're lonely, Jane. I've told you a hundred times that you ought to make friends for yourself."

"Oh, I don't care for that. I don't want friends, not many friends. These acting people, they're not real folks. I don't savvy their ways and they don't savvy mine. They always end by disliking me because I'm queer and different from them. You have been my friend, and your wife — that is, she used to be." Suddenly Jane became more her usual self and spoke with childlike wistfulness. "She does n't come to see me any more, Mr. Morena. And I could love her. She's so like a little girl with those round eyes —" Jane held up two circles made by forefingers and thumbs to represent Betty's round eyes. "Oh, dear!" she said; "is n't she awfully winning? Seems as if you must be taking care of her. She's so small and fine."

Jasper laughed with some bitterness.

"She does n't like me now," sighed Jane, but the feelings Betty had hurt were connected with a later development so that they turned her mood and brought her to a more normal dejection. She was no longer a caged beast, she had temporarily forgotten her bars.

"I think you're wrong," said Jasper doubtfully. "Betty does like you. She's merely busy and preoccupied. I've been neglected myself."

Jane gave him a far too expressive look. It was as though she had said, "You don't fancy that she cares for you?"

Jasper flushed and blinked his long, Oriental eyes.

"It's a pity you have n't a lover, Jane," he said.

She had walked over to the window, and his speech, purposely a trifle cruel and insulting, did not make her turn.

"You're angry," she said. "You'd better go home. I'm not in good humor myself."

At which he laughed his murmuring, musical laugh and prepared to leave her.

"I have a great deal of courage," he said, getting into his coat, "to bring a wild-cat here, chain her up, and tease her — eh?"

"You think you have me chained?" Her tone was enraged and scornful. "I can snap your flimsy little tether and go."

She wheeled upon him. She looked tall and fierce and free.

"No, no," he cried with deprecating voice and gesture. "You are making Mr. Luck's fortune and mine, not to mention your own. You must n't break your chains. Get used to them. We all have to, you know. It's much the best method."

"I shall never get used to this life, never. It just — somehow — is n't mine."

"Perhaps when you meet Mr. Luck, he'll be able to reconcile you."

Her expressive face darkened. "When shall I meet Mr. Luck?"

"Soon, I hope. Mr. Melton knows just when to announce the authorship."

"I hate Mr. Luck more than any one in the world," she said in a low, quiet voice.

Jasper stared. "Hate him! Why, in the name of savagery, should you hate him?"

"Oh, I can't explain. But you'd better keep us apart. How came he to write 'The Leopardess'?"

"I shall leave him to tell you that. Good-night."

CHAPTER IX

GRAY ENVELOPES

IT was with more than the usual sinking of heart that Jasper let himself that evening into the beautiful house which Betty and he called their home. Joan's too expressive look had stung the old soreness of his disillusionment. He knew that the house was empty of welcome. He took off his hat and coat dejectedly. There were footsteps of his man who came from the far end of the hall.

While he stood waiting, Jasper noticed the absence of a familiar fragrance. For the first time in years Betty had forgotten to order flowers. The red roses which Jasper always caressed with a long, appreciative finger as he went by the table in the hall, were missing. Their absence gave him a faint sensation of alarm.

"Mr. Kane, Mrs. Morena's brother, has called to see you, sir. He is waiting."

Jasper's eyebrows rose. "To see me? Is he with Mrs. Morena now?"

"No, sir. Mrs. Morena went out this morning and has not yet returned. Mr. Kane has been here since five o'clock, sir."

"Very well."

It was a mechanical speech of dismissal. The footman went off. Jasper stood tapping his chin with his finger. Woodward Kane come to see him during Betty's absence! Woodward had not spoken more than three or four icy words of necessity to him since the marriage. After a stiff, ungracious fashion this brother had befriended Betty, but to his Jewish brother-in-law he had shown only a slightly disguised distaste. The Jew was well used to such a manner. He treated it with light bitterness, but he did not love to receive the users of it in his own house. It was with heightened color and bent brows that he pushed apart the long, crimson hangings and came into the immense drawing-room.

It was softly lighted and pleasantly warmed. A fire burned. The tall, fair visitor rose from a seat near the blaze and turned all in one rigid piece toward his advancing host. Jasper was perfectly conscious that his own gesture and speech of greeting were too eager, too ingratiating, that they had a touch of servility. He hated them himself, but they were inherited with his blood, as instinctive as the wagging of a dog's tail. They were met by a precise bow, no smile, no taking of his outstretched hand.

Jasper drew himself up at once, put the slighted hand on the back of a tall, crimson-damask chair, and looked his stateliest and most handsome self.

"Betty has n't come in yet," he said. "You've been waiting for her?"

Woodward Kane pulled at his short, yellow mustache and stared at Jasper with his large, blank, blue eyes. "As a matter of fact I did n't call to see my sister, but to see you. I have just come from Elizabeth. She is at my house. She came to me this morning."

Jasper's fingers tightened on the chair. "She is sick?"

"No." There was a pause during which the blank, blue eyes staring at him slowly gathered a look of cold pleasure. Jasper was aware that this man who hated him was enjoying his present mission.

"Shall we sit down? I shall have to take a good deal of your time, I am afraid. There is rather a good deal to be gone over."

Jasper sat down in the chair the back of which he had been holding. "Will you smoke?" he asked, and smiled his charming smile.

There was now not a trace of embarrassment, anger, or anxiety about him. His eyes were quiet, his voice flexible. Woodward declined to smoke, crossed his beautifully clothed legs and drew a small gray envelope from his pocket. Jasper's eyes fastened upon it at once. It was Betty's paper and her angular, boyish writing marched across it. Evidently the note was addressed to him. He waited while Woodward turned it about in his long, stiff, white fingers.

"About two months ago Betty came to me one evening in great distress of mind. She asked for my advice and to the best of my ability I gave it to her. I wish that she had asked for it ten years ago. She might have saved herself a great deal. This time she has not only asked for it, but she has been following it, and, in following it, she has now left your house and come to mine. This, of course, will not surprise you."

"It does, however, surprise me greatly." It was still the gentle murmur, but Jasper's cigarette smoke veiled his face.

"I cannot understand that. However, it's not my business. Betty has asked me to interview you to-day so that she may be spared the humiliation. After this, you must address your communications to her lawyers. In a short time Rogers and Daring will serve you with notice of divorce."

Jasper sat perfectly still, leaning slightly forward, his cigarette between his fingers.

"So-o!" he said after a long silence. Then he held out his hand. "I may have Betty's letter?"

Woodward Kane withheld it and again that look of pleasure was visible in his eyes. "Just a moment, please. I should like to have my own say out first. I shall have to be brutal, I am afraid. In these matters there is nothing for it but frankness. Your infidelity has been common talk for some time. The story of it first came to Betty's ears on the evening when she came to me two months ago. Since then there has been but one possible course."

Jasper kept another silence, more difficult, however, than his last. His pallor was noticeable. "You say my — infidelity is common talk. There has been a name used?"

"Your protégée from Wyoming — Jane West."

Jasper was on his feet, and Woodward too rose, jerkily holding up a hand. "No excitement, please," he begged. "Let us conduct this unfortunate interview like gentlemen, if possible."

Jasper laughed. "As you say — if possible. Why, man, it was Betty who helped me bring Miss West to New York, it was Betty who helped me to install her here, it was Betty who chose the furnishings for her apartment, who helped her buy her clothes, who engaged her maid, who gave her most of her training. This is the most preposterous, the most filthy perversion of the truth. Betty must know it better than any one else. Come, now, Woodward, there's something more in it than this?" Jasper had himself in hand, but it was easy now to see the effort it cost him. The veins of his forehead were swollen.

"I shall not discuss the matter with you. Betty has excellent evidence, unimpeachable witnesses. There is no doubt in my mind, nor in the minds of her lawyers, that she will win her suit and get her divorce, her release. Of course, you will not contest —"

Jasper stopped in his pacing which had begun to take the curious, circling, weaving form characteristic of him, and, standing now with his head thrown back, he spoke sonorously.

"Do you imagine for one instant, Kane, — does Betty imagine for one instant, — that I shall not contest?"

This changed the look of cold pleasure in Woodward's eyes, which grew blank again. "Do you mean me to understand — Naturally, I took it for granted that you would act as most gentlemen act under the circumstances."

"Then you have taken too much for granted, you and Betty. Ten years ago your sister gave herself to me. She is mine. I will not for a whim, for a passion, for a temporary alienation, let her go. Neither will I have my good name and the name of a good woman besmirched for the sake of this impertinent desire for a release. I love my wife" — his voice was especially Hebraic and especially abhorrent to the other — "and as a husband I mean to keep her from the ruin this divorce would mean to her —"

"Far from being her ruin, Morena, it would be the saving of her. Her ruin was as nearly as possible brought about ten years ago, when against the advice, against the wishes of every one who loved her, she made her insane marriage with an underbred, commercial, and licentious Jew. She was seventeen and you seized your opportunity."

Jasper had stepped close. He was a head taller and several inches broader of shoulder than his brother-in-law. "As long as you are in my house, don't insult me. I am, as you say, a Jew, and I am, as you say, of a commercial family. But I am not, I have never been licentious. Is it necessary to use such language? You suggested that this interview be conducted by us like gentlemen."

"The man who refuses to give her liberty to a wife that loathes him, scarcely comes under the definition."

"My ideas on the matter are different. We need not discuss them. If you will let me read my wife's letter, I think that we can come to an end of this."

Woodward unwillingly surrendered the small, gray envelope to a quivering, outstretched hand. Jasper turned away and stood near the lamp. But his excitement prevented him from reading. The angular writing jumped before his eyes. At last, the words straightened themselves.

I am glad that you have given me this opportunity to escape from a life that for a long time has been dreadful to me. Ten years ago I made a disaster of my life and yours. Forgive me if you can and let me escape. I will not see you again. Whatever you may have to say, please say it to Woodward. From now on he is my protector. In other matters there are my lawyers. It is absolutely not to be thought of that I should speak to you. I hope never to see you alone. I want you to hate me and this note ought to make it easy for you.

BETTY

Jasper stared at the name. He was utterly bewildered, utterly staggered, by the amazing dissimulation practiced by this small, soft-lipped, round-eyed girl who had lived with him for so long, sufficiently pliable, sufficiently agreeable. What was back of it all? Another man, of course. In imagination he was examining the faces of his acquaintances, narrowing his lids as though the real men passed in review before him.

"Perhaps you understand the situation better now?" asked Woodward cruelly.

Jasper's intense pain and humiliation gave him a sort of calm. He seemed entirely cool when he moved back toward his brother-in-law; his eyes were clear, the heat had gone from his temples. He was even smiling a little, though there was a white, even frame to his lips.

"I shall not write to Betty nor attempt to see her," he said quietly. "But I shall ask you to take a message to her."

Woodward assented.

"Tell her she shall have her release, but to get it she will have to walk through the mire and there will be no one waiting for her on the other side. Can you remember that? Not even you will be there." He was entirely self-assured so that Woodward felt a chill of dismay.

"I shall contest the suit," went on Jasper, "and I believe that I shall win it. You may tell Betty so if you like or she can wait to hear it from my lawyer." He put the envelope into his pocket, crossed the room, and held back one of the crimson curtains of the door.

"If you have nothing more to say," he smiled, "neither have I. Good-bye."

He bowed slightly, and Woodward found himself passing before him in silence and some confusion. He stood for a moment in the hall and, having stammered his way to a cold "Good-afternoon," he put on his hat and went out.

Jasper returned to the empty drawing-room and began his weaving march.

Before he could begin his spinning which he hoped would entangle Betty and leave her powerless for him to hold or to release at will, he must go to Jane West and tell her what trick life with his help had played upon her. The prospect was bitterly distasteful. Jasper accused himself of selfishness. Because she cared nothing for the world, was a creature apart, he had let the world think what it would. He knew that an askance look would not hurt her; for himself, secure in innocence, he did not care; for Betty, he had thought her cruelly certain of him.

He went to Jane the day after his interview with Woodward Kane. It was Sunday afternoon. She was out, but came in very soon, and he stood up to meet her with an air of confusion and guilt.

"What's the matter with you?" she asked, pulling her gloves from her long hands.

Her quickly observant eyes swept him. She walked to him and stood near. The frosty air was still about her and her face was lightly stung to color with exercise. Her wild eyes were startling under the brim of her smart, tailored hat.

Jasper put a hand on either of her shoulders and bent his head before her. "My poor child — if I'd only left you in your kitchen!"

Joan tightened her lips, then smiled uncertainly. "You've got me scared," she said, stepped back and sat down, her hands in her muff. "What is it?" she asked; and in that moment of waiting she was sickly reminded of other moments in her life — of the nearing sound of Pierre's webs on a crystal winter night, of the sound of Prosper's footsteps going away from her up the mountain trail on a swordlike, autumn morning.

Jasper began his pacing. Feeling carefully for delicate phrases, he told her Betty's accusation, of her purpose.

Joan took off her hat, pushed back the hair from her forehead; then, as he came to the end, she looked up at him. Her pupils were larger than usual and the light, frosty tint of rose had left her cheeks.

"Would you mind telling me that again?" she asked.

He did so, more explicitly.

"She thinks, Betty thinks, that I have been — that we have been —? She thinks that of me? No wonder she has n't been coming to see me!" She stopped, staring blindly at him; then, "You must tell her it is n't true," she said pitifully, and the quiver of her lips hurt him.

"Ah! But she does n't want to believe that, my dear. She wants to believe the worst. It is her opportunity to escape me."

"Have n't you loved her? Have you hurt her?" asked Joan.

"God knows I have loved her. I have never hurt her — consciously. Even she cannot think that I have."

"Why must she blame me? Why do I have to be brought into this, Mr. Morena? Can't she go away from you? Why do the lawyers have to take it up? You are unhappy, and I am so sorry. But you would n't want her to stay if — if she does n't love you?"

"I want her. I mean to keep her or — break her." He turned his back to say this and went toward the window. Joan, fascinated, watched his fingers working into one another, tightening, crushing. "It's another man she wants," he said hoarsely, "and if I can prevent it, she shall not have him. I will force her to keep her vows to me — force her. If it kills her, I'll break this passion, this fancy. I'll have her back —" He wheeled round, showing a twitching face. "I'll prove her infidelity whether she's been unfaithful or not, and then I'll take her back, after the world has given her one of its names —"

"You don't love her," said Joan, very white. "You want to brand her."

"By God!" swore the Jew, "and I will brand her. I'll brand her."

He fumbled in his pocket and brought out the small envelope Woodward Kane had handed to him the day before. He stood turning the letter about in his hands as though some such meaningless occupation was a necessity to him. Joan's eyes, falling upon the letter, widened and fixed.

"She has written to me," said Jasper. "She wants her liberty. She wants it in such a way that she will fly clear and I — yes, and you, too, will be left in the mud. There's a man somewhere, of course. She thinks she has evidence, witnesses against me. I don't know what rubbish she has got together. But I'm going to fight her. I'm going to win. I'll save you if I can, Jane; if not, of course I am at your service for any amends —"

He stopped in his halting speech, for Joan had stood up and was moving across the room, her eyes fastened on the letter in his hands. She had the air of a sleep-walker.

She opened a drawer of her desk, took out an old tin box, once used for tobacco, and drew forth a small, gray envelope torn in two. Then she came back to him and said, "Let me see that letter," and he obeyed as though she had the right to ask.

She took his letter and hers and compared the two, the small, gray squares lying unopened on her knee, and she spoke incomprehensibly.

"Betty is 'the tall child,'" she said, and laughed with a catch in her breath.

Jasper looked at the envelopes. They were identical; Betty's gray note-paper crossed by Betty's angular, upright hand, very bold, very black. The torn envelope was addressed to Prosper Gael. Jasper took it, opened each half, laid the parts together, and read:

Jasper is dying. By the time you get this he will be dead. If you can forgive me for having failed you in courage last year, come back. What I have been to you before I will be again, only, this time, we can love openly. Come back.

"Jane," — Morena spoke brokenly, — "what does it mean?"

"He built that cabin in Wyoming for her," said Joan, speaking as though Jasper had seen the cañon hiding-place and known its history, "and she did n't come. He brought me there on his sled. I was hurt. I was terribly hurt. He took care of me —"

"Prosper?" Jasper thrust in. His face was drawn with excitement.

"Yes. Prosper Gael. I was there with him for months. At first I was n't strong enough to go away, and then, after a while, I tried. But I was too lonely and sorrowful. In the spring I loved him. I thought I loved him. He wanted me. I was all alone in the world. I did n't know that he loved another woman. I thought she was dead — like Pierre. Prosper had clothes for her there. I suppose — I've thought it out since — that she was to leave as if for a short journey, and then secretly go on that long one, and she could n't take many things with her. So he had beautiful stuffs for her — and a little suit to wear in the snow. That's how I came to call her 'the tall child,' seeing that little suit, long and narrow. . . . This letter came one morning, one awfully bright morning. He read it and went out and the next day he went away. Afterwards I found the letter torn in two beside his desk on the floor. I took it and I've always kept it. 'The tall child'! He looked so terrible when I called her that. . . . And she was your Betty all the time!"

"Yes," said Morena slowly. "She was my Betty all the time." He gave her a twisted smile and put the two papers carefully into an inside pocket. "I am going to keep this letter, Jane. Truly the ways of the Lord are past finding out."

Joan looked at him in growing uneasiness. Her mind, never quick to take in all the bearings and the consequences of her acts, was beginning to work. "What are you going to do with it, Mr. Morena? I don't want you to do Betty a hurt. She must have loved Prosper Gael. Perhaps she still loves him."

This odd appeal drew another difficult smile from Betty's husband. "Quite obviously she still loves him, Jane. She is divorcing me so that she can marry him."

"But, Mr. Morena, I don't believe he will marry her now. He is tired of her. He is that kind of lover. He gets tired. Now he would like to marry me. He told me so. Perhaps — if Betty knew that — she might come back to you, without your branding her."

Jasper was startled out of his vengeful stillness.

"Prosper Gael wants to marry you? He has told you so?"

"Yes." She was sad and humbled. "*Now* he wants to marry me and once he told me things about marrying. He said" — Joan quoted slowly, her eyes half-closed in Prosper's manner, her voice a musical echo of his thin, vibrant tone — "'It's man's most studied insult to woman.'"

"Yes. That's Prosper," murmured Jasper.

"I would n't marry him, Mr. Morena, even if I could — not if I were to be — burnt for refusing him."

Jasper looked probingly at her, a new speculation in his eyes. She had begun to fit definitely into his plans. It seemed there might be a way to frustrate Betty and to keep a hold upon his valuable protégée. "Are you so sure of that, Jane?"

"Ah!" she answered; "you doubt it because I once thought I loved him? But you don't know all about me . . ."

He stood silent, busy with his weaving. At last he looked at her rather blankly, impersonally. Joan was conscious of a frightened, lonely chill. She put out her hand uncertainly, a wrinkle appearing sharp and deep between her eyes.

"Mr. Morena, please — I have n't any one but you. I don't understand very well what this divorcing rightly means. Nor what they will do to me. Will you be thinking of me a little? I would n't ask it, for I know you are unhappy and bothered enough, but, you see —"

He did not notice the hand. "It will come out right, Jane. Don't worry," he said with absent gentleness. "Keep your mind on your work. I'll look out for your best interests. Be sure of that." He came near to her, his hat in his hand, ready to go. "Try to forget all about it, will you?"

"Oh, I can't do that. I feel sort of — burnt. Betty thinking — that! But I'll do my work just the same, of course."

She sighed heavily and sat, the unnoticed hand clasped in its fellow.

When he had gone she called nervously for her maid. She had a hitherto unknown dread of being alone. But when Mathilde, chosen by Betty, came with her furtive step and treacherous eyes, Joan invented some duty for her. It occurred to her that Mathilde might be one of Betty's witnesses. For some time the girl's watchfulness and intrusions had become irritatingly noticeable. And Morena was Joan's only frequent and informal visitor.

"Mathilde thinks I am — *that!*" Joan said to herself; and afterwards, with a burst of weeping, "And, of course, that is what I am." Her past sin pressed upon her and she trembled, remembering Pierre's wistful, seeking face. If he should find her now, he would find her branded, indeed — now he could never believe that she had indeed been innocent of guilt in the matter of Holliwell. Her father had first put a mark upon her. Since then the world had only deepened his revenge.

There followed a sleepless, dry, and aching night.

CHAPTER X

THE SPIDER

HULLO. Is this Mrs. Morena?"

Betty held the receiver languidly. Her face had grown very thin and her eyes were patient. They were staring now absently through the front window of Woodward Kane's sitting-room at a day of driving April rain.

"Yes. This is Mrs. Morena."

The next speech changed her into a flushed and palpitating girl.

"Mr. Gael wishes to know, madam," — the man-servant recited his lesson automatically, — "if you have seen the exhibition of Foster's water-colors, Fifty-eighth Street and Fifth Avenue. He wants to know if you will be there this afternoon at five o'clock. No. 88 in the inner room is the picture he would especially like you to notice, madam."

Betty's hand and voice were trembling.

"No. I have n't seen it." She hesitated, looking at the downpour. "Tell him, please, that I will be there."

Her voice trailed off doubtfully.

The man at the other end clipped out a "Very well, madam," and hung up.

Betty was puzzled. Why had Prosper sent her this message, made this appointment by his servant? Perhaps because he was afraid that, in her exaggerated caution, she might refuse to meet him if she could explain to him the reason for her refusal, or gauge the importance of his request. With a servant she could do neither, and the very uncertainty would force her to accept. It was a dreadful day. Nobody would be out, certainly not at the tea-hour, to look at Foster's pictures — an insignificant exhibition. Betty felt triumphant. At last, this far too acquiescent lover had rebelled against her decree of silence and separation.

At five o'clock she stepped out of her taxicab, made a run for shelter, and found herself in the empty exhibition rooms. She checked her wrap and her umbrella, took a catalogue from the little table, chatted for a moment with the man in charge, then moved about, looking carelessly at the pictures. No. 88 in the inner room! Her heart was beating violently, the hand in her muff was cold. She went slowly toward the inner room and saw at once that, under a small canvas at its far end, Prosper stood waiting for her.

He waited even after he had seen her smile and quickening step, and when he did come forward, it was with obvious reluctance. Betty's smile faded. His face was haggard and grim, unlike itself; his eyes lack-luster as she had never seen them. This was not the face of an impatient lover. It was — she would not name it, but she was conscious of a feeling of angry sickness.

He took her hand and forced a smile.

"Betty, I thought you disapproved of this kind of thing. I think, myself, it's rather imprudent to arrange a meeting through your maid."

Betty jerked away her hand, drew a sharp breath. "What do you mean? I did n't arrange this meeting. It was you — your man."

They became simultaneously aware of a trap. It had sprung upon them. With the look of trapped things, they stared at each other, and Betty instinctively looked back over her shoulder. There stood Jasper in the doorway of the room. He looked like the most casual of visitors to an art-gallery, he carried a catalogue in his hand. When he saw that he was seen he smiled easily and came over to them.

"You will have to forgive me," he murmured pleasantly; "you see, it was necessary to see you both together and Betty is not willing to allow me an interview. I am sorry to have chosen a public place and to have used a trick to get you here, but I could not think of any other plan. This is really private enough. I have arranged this exhibition for Foster and it is closed to the public to-day. We got in by special permit — a fact you probably missed. And, after all, civilized people ought to be able to talk about anything without excitement."

Betty's eyes glared at him. "I will not stay! This is insufferable!"

But he put out his hand and something in his gesture compelled her. She sat down on the round, plush seat in the middle of the room and looked up at the two men helplessly. Joan had once leaned in a doorway, silent and unconsulted, while two men, her father and Pierre, settled their property rights in her. Betty was, after all, in no better case. She listened, whiter and whiter, till at the last she slowly raised her muff and pressed it against her twisted mouth.

Morena stood with his hand resting on the high back of the circular seat almost directly above Betty's head. It seemed to hold her there like a bar. But it was at Prosper he looked, to Prosper he spoke. "My friend," he began, and the accentuation of the Hebraic quality of his voice had an instantaneous effect upon his two listeners. Both Prosper and Betty knew he was master of some intense agitation. They were conscious of an increasing rapidity of their pulses. "My friend, I thought that I knew you fairly well, as one man knows another, but I find that there have been certain limits to my knowledge. How extraordinary it is! This inner world of our own lives which we keep closely to ourselves! I have a friend, yes, a very good friend, a very dear friend," — the ironic insistence upon this word gave Prosper the shock of a repeated blow, — "and I fancy, in the ignorance of my conceit, that this friend's life is sufficiently open to my understanding. I see him leave college, I see him go out on various adventures. I share with him, by letters and confidences, thc excitement of these adventures. I know with regret that he suffers from ill-health and goes West, and there, with a great deal of sympathy, I imagine him living, drearily enough, in some small, health-giving Western town, writing his book and later his play which he has so generously allowed me to produce."

"What the devil are you after, Jasper?"

"But I do my friend an injustice," went on the manager, undiverted. "His career is infinitely more romantic. He has built himself a little log house amongst the mountains, and he has decorated it and laid in a supply of dainty and exquisite stuffs. I believe that there is even an outing suit, small and narrow —"

"My God!" said Prosper, very low.

There was a silence. Jasper moved slightly, and Prosper started, but the Jew stayed in his former place, only that he bent his head a little, half-closed his eyes, and marked time with the hand that was not buried in the plush above Betty's head. He recited in a heavy voice, and it was here that Betty raised her muff!

> Jasper is dying. By the time you get this letter he will be dead. If you can forgive me for having failed in courage last year, come back. What I have been to you before, I will be to you again, only this time we can love openly. Come back.

"I am going mad!" said Prosper harshly, and indeed his face had a pinched, half-crazy look.

The Jew waved his hand. "Oh, no, no, no. It is only that you are making a discovery. Letters should be burnt, my friend, not torn and thrown away, but burnt." He stood up to his stateliest height and he made a curious and rather terrible gesture of breaking something between his two hands. "I have this letter and I hold you and Betty — so!" he said softly — "so!"

Betty spoke. "I might have told you that I loved him, that I have loved him for years, Jasper. If you use this evidence, if you bring this counter-suit, it will bring about the same, the very same, result. Prosper and I —" She broke off choking.

"Of course. Betty and I will be married at once, as soon as she gets her divorce, or you get yours." But Prosper's voice was hollow and strained.

"You will be married, Betty," went on Jasper as calmly as before; "you, branded in the eyes of the world as an unfaithful wife, will be married to a man who has ceased to love you."

"That is not true," said Betty.

"Look at his face, my dear. Look at it carefully. Now, watch it closely. Prosper Gael, if I should tell that with a little patience, a little skill, a little unselfishness, you could win a certain woman who once loved you — eh? — a certain Jane West, could you bring yourself to marry this discarded wife of mine?"

Betty sprang up and caught Prosper's arm in her small hand.

"He is tired of you, Betty. He loves Jane

West." Jasper laughed shortly, looking at the tableau they made: Prosper white, caught in the teeth of honor, his face set to hide its secret, Betty reading his eyes, his soul.

"I am entirely yours, in your hands," said Prosper Gael.

Betty shook his arm and let it go. "You are lying. You love the woman. Do you think I can't see?"

"It will be a very strange divorce suit," went on Jasper. "Your lawyers, Betty, will perhaps prove your case. My lawyers will certainly prove mine, and, when we find ourselves free, our — our lovers will then unite in holy matrimony — rather an original outcome."

"Will you go, Prosper?" asked Betty. It was a command.

He saw that, at that moment, his presence was intolerable to her.

"Of course. If you wish it. Jasper, you know where to find me, and, Betty," — he turned to her with a weary tenderness, — "forgive me and make use of me, if you will, as you will."

He went out quickly, feeling himself a coward to leave her, knowing that he would be a coward to stay to watch the anguish of her broken heart and pride. For an instant he did hesitate and look back. They were standing together, calmly, man and wife. What could he do to help them, he that had broken their lives?

Betty turned to Jasper, still with the muff before her mouth, looking at him above it with her wide, childlike, desperate eyes.

"What do you get out of this, Jasper? I will go to Woodward. I will never come back to you. . . . Is it revenge?"

"If so," said Jasper, "it is n't yet complete. Betty, you have been rash to pit yourself against me. You must have known that I would break you utterly. I will break you, my dear, and I will have you back, and I will be your master instead of your servant, and I will love you —"

"You must be mad. I'm afraid of you. Please let me go."

"In a moment, when you have learned what home you have to go to. This morning I had an interview with your brother in his office, and he wrote this letter that I have in my pocket and asked me to give it to you."

Betty laid down her muff, showing at last the pale and twisted mouth. Jasper watched her read her brother's letter, and his eyes were as patient and observant as the eyes of a skillful doctor who has given a dangerous but necessary draught.

Betty read the small, sharp, careful writing, very familiar to her.

I have instructed your maid to pack your things and to return at once to your husband's house. He is a much too merciful man. You have treated him shamelessly. I can find no excuse for you. My house is definitely closed to you. I will send you no money, allow you no support, countenance you in no way. This is final. You have only one course, to return humbly and with penitence to your husband, submit yourself to him, and learn to love and honor and obey him as he deserves. The evidence of your guilt is incontrovertible. I utterly disbelieve your story against him. It is part of your sin, and it is easily to be explained in the light of my present knowledge of your real character. Whether you return to Morena or not, I emphatically reassert that I will not see you or speak to you again. You are to my mind a woman of shameless life, such a woman as I should feel justified in turning out of any decent household.

WOODWARD KANE

The room turned giddily about Betty. She saw the whole roaring city turn about her, and she knew that there was no home in it for her. She could go to Prosper Gael, but at what horrible sacrifice of pride, and, if Jasper now refused to bring suit, could she ask this man, who no longer loved her, to keep her as his mistress? What could she do? Where could she turn? How could she keep herself alive? For the first time, life, stripped of everything but its hard and ugly bones, faced her. She had always been sheltered, been dependent, been loved. Once before she had lost courage and had failed to venture beyond the familiar shelter of custom and convention. Now, she was again most horribly afraid. Anything was better than this feeling of being lost, alone. She looked at Jasper. At that moment he was nothing but a protector, a means of life, and he knew it.

"Will you come home with me now?" he asked her bitterly.

Betty forced the twisted mouth to speech. "What else is there for me to do?" she said.

CHAPTER XI

THE CLEAN WILD THING

"THE Reverend Francis Holliwell." Morena turned the card over and over in his hand. "Holliwell. Holliwell. Frank Holliwell." Yes. One of the fellows that had dropped out. Big, athletic youngster; left college in his junior year and studied for the ministry. Fine chap. Popular. Especially decent to him when he had begun to play that difficult rôle of a man without a country. Now here was the card of the Reverend Francis Holliwell and the man himself, no doubt, waiting below. Jasper tried to remember. He'd heard something about Frank. Oh, yes. The young clergyman had given up a fashionable parish in the East — small Norman church, wealthy parishioners, splendid stipend, beautiful stone Norman rectory — thrown it all up to go West on some unheard-of mission in the sage-brush. He was back now, probably for money, donations wanted for a building, church or hospital or library. Jasper in imagination wrote out a generous check. Before going down he glanced at the card again and noticed some lines across the back:

This is to introduce one of my best friends, Pierre Landis, of Wyoming. Please be of service to him. His mission has and deserves to have my full sympathy.

So, after all, it was n't Holliwell below and the check-book would not be needed. "Pierre Landis, of Wyoming." Jasper went down the stairs and on the way he remembered a letter received from Yarnall a long time before. He remembered it with an accession of alarm. "I've probably let hell loose for your protégée, Jane; given your address, and incidentally hers, to a fellow who wants her pretty badly. His name's Pierre Landis. You're a pretty good judge of white men. Size him up and do what's best for Jane."

For some time after receiving this letter, Jasper had expected the appearance of this Pierre Landis, then had forgotten him. The fellow who wanted Jane so badly had been a long while on his way to her. Remembering and wondering, the manager opened the crimson curtains and stepped into the presence of Pierre.

Even if he had had no foreknowledge, Jasper felt that, at sight of his visitor, his fancy would have jumped to Joan. It was the eyes; he had seen no others but hers like them for clarity; far-seeing, grave eyes that held a curious depth of light. Here was one of Joan's kindred, one of the clean, wild things.

Then came the gentle Western drawl. "I'm right sorry to trouble you, Mr. Morena."

Jasper took a brown hand that had the feel of iron. The man's face, on a level with Jasper's, was very brown and lean. It had a worn look, a trifle desperate, perhaps, in the lines of lip and the expression of the smoke-colored eyes. Jasper, sensitive to undercurrents, became aware that he stood in some fashion for a forlorn hope in the life of this Pierre. At the same time the manager remembered a confidence of Jane's. She had been "afraid of some one." She had been running away. There was one that must n't find her, and to run away from him, that was the business of her life. Pierre Landis was this "one," the something wild and clean that had at last come searching even into this city. It was necessary that Jane's present protector should be very careful. There must be no running away this time, and Pierre must be warned off. Jasper had plans of his own for his star player. For one thing she must draw Prosper Gael completely out of Betty's life.

Jasper made his guest comfortable, sat opposite to him, and lighted a cigarette. Although

Pierre had accepted one, he did not smoke. He was far too disturbed.

"Frank Holliwell gave me a note to you, Mr. Morena. I got your address some years ago from Yarnall, of Lazy-Y Ranch, Middle Fork, Wyoming. I've been gettin' my affairs into shape ever since, so that I could come East. I don't rightly know whether Yarnall would have wrote to you concernin' me or no."

"Yes. He did write — just a line — two years ago."

Pierre studied his own long, brown hands, turning the soft hat between them. When he lifted his eyes, they were intensely blue. It was as though blue fire had consumed the smoke.

"I've been takin' after a girl. She was called Jane on Yarnall's ranch an' she was cook there for the outfit. Nobody knowed her story nor her name. She left the mornin' I came in an' I did n't set eyes on her. You were takin' her East to teach her to play-act for you. I don't know whether you done so or not, but I've come here to learn where she is so that I can find out if she's the woman I'm lookin' for."

Morena smiled kindly. "You've come a long way, Mr. Landis, on an uncertainty."

"Yes. sir." Pierre did not smile. He was holding himself steady. "But I'm used to uncertainty. There ain't no uncertainty that can keep me from seekin' after the person I want." He paused, the eyes still fixed upon Morena, who, uncomfortable under them, veiled himself thinly in cigarette smoke. "I want to see this Jane," Pierre ended gently.

"Nothing easier, Landis. I'll give you a ticket to 'The Leopardess.' She is acting the title part. She is my leading lady and a very extraordinary young actress. Of course, it's none of my business, but in a way I am Miss West's guardian —"

"Miss West?"

"Yes. That is Jane's name — Jane West. You think it is an assumed one?"

Pierre stood up. "I'm not thinkin' on this trip," he said; "I'm hopin'."

"I am sorry, but I am afraid you're on the wrong track. There may be a resemblance, there may even be a marked resemblance, between Miss West and the person you want to find, but — again please forgive me — I am in the place of guardian to her at present and I should like to know something of your business, enough of it, that is, to be sure that your sudden appearance, if you happen to be right in your surmise, won't frighten my leading lady out of her wits and send her off to Kalamazoo on the next train."

Pierre evidently resented the fashion of this speech. "I'm sorry," he said with dignity, "not to be able to tell you anything. I'll be careful not to frighten Miss West. I can see her first from a distance an' then —"

"Certainly. Certainly."

Jasper rang and directed his man to get an envelope from an upstairs table. When it came, he handed it to Pierre.

"That is a ticket for to-morrow night's performance. It's the best seat I can give you, though it is not very near the stage. However, you will certainly be able to recognize your — Jane, if she is your Jane."

Pierre pocketed the ticket. "Thank you," he murmured. His face was expressionless.

Jasper was making rapid plans. "Oh, by the way," he said hurriedly, "if you should stand near the stage exit to-night, say at about twelve o'clock, you could see Miss West come out and get into her motor. That would give you a fairly close view. But even if you find you are mistaken, Landis, be sure to see 'The Leopardess.' It's well worth your while. You're going? Won't you dine with me to-night?"

"No, thank you. I would n't be carin' to to-night. I — I reckon I've got this matter too much on my mind. Thank you very much, Mr. Morena."

"Before you go, tell me about Holliwell. He was a good friend of mine."

"He was a good friend to most every one he knowed. He was more than that to me."

"Then he's been a success out there?"

Pierre meditated over the words. "Success? Why, yes, I reckon he's been all of that."

"A difficult mission, is n't it? Trying to bring you fellows to God?"

Pierre smiled. "I reckon we get closer to God out there than you do here. We sure get the fear of Him even if we don't get nothin' else. When you fight winter an' all outdoors an' come near to death with hosses an' what-not, why, I guess you're gettin' close to *somethin'* not quite to be explained. Holliwell, he's a first-class sin-buster, best I ever knowed."

Morena laughed. He was beginning to enjoy his visitor. "Sin-buster?"

"That's one name fer a parson. Well, sir, I guess Holliwell is plumb close to bein' a prize devil-twister."

"Tell me how you first met him. It ought to be a good story."

But the young man's face grew bleak at this. "It ain't a good story, sir," he said grimly. "It ain't anything like that. I must wish you good-by, an' thank you kindly."

"But you'll let me see you again? Where are you stopping? Holliwell's friends are mine."

Pierre gave him the address of a small, down-town hotel, thanked him again, and, standing in the hall, added, "If I'm wrong in the notion that brought me to New York, I'll be goin' back again to my ranch, Mr. Morena. I'm goin' back to ranchin' on the old homestead. I've got it fixed up." He seemed to look through Jasper into an enormous distance. Morena was almost un-cannily aware of the long, long journey by which this man's spirit had trodden, of the desert he faced ahead of him if the search must fail. Was it wrong to warn Jane? Ought this man to be given his chance? Surely here stood before him Jane's mate. Jasper wished that he knew more of the history back of Pierre and the girl. A man could do little but look out for his own interests, when he worked in the dark. Which would be the better man for Jane? — this Jane so trained, so educated, so far removed superficially from the ungrammatical, bronzed, clumsily dressed, graceful visitor. In every worldly respect, doubtless,

Prosper Gael. Only — there were Pierre's eyes and the soul looking out of them.

Jasper said good-bye half-absently.

An hour later he went to call on Jane.

He found her done up in an apron and a dust-cap cleaning house with astonishing spirit. She and the Bridget, who had recently been substituted for Mathilde, were merry. Bridget was sitting on the sill, her upper half shut out, her round, brick-colored face laughing through the pane she was polishing. Jane was up a ladder, dusting books.

She came down to greet Morena, and he saw regretfully the sad change in her face and bearing which his arrival caused. Bridget was sent to the kitchen. Jane made apologies, and sitting on the ladder step she looked up at him with the look of some one who expects a blow.

"What is it now, Mr. Morena? Have the lawyers begun to —"

He had purposely kept her in the dark, purposely neglected her, left her to loneliness, in the hope of furthering the purposes of Prosper Gael.

"I have n't come to discuss that, Jane. Soon I hope to have good news for you. But to-day I've come to give you a hint — a warning, in fact —

to prepare you for what I am sure will be a shock."

"Yes?" She was flushed and breathing fast. Her fingers were busy with the feather-duster on her knee and her eyes were still waiting.

"I had a visitor this morning — Pierre Landis, of Wyoming."

She rose, came to him, and clutched his arm. "Pierre? Pierre?" She looked around her, wild as a captured bird. "Oh, I must go! I must go!"

"Jane, my child," — he put his arm about her, held her two hands in his, — "you must do nothing of the kind. If you don't want this Pierre to find you, if you don't want him to come into your life, there's an easy, a very simple, way to put an end to his pursuit. Don't you know that?"

She stared up at him, quivering in his arm. "No. What is it? How can I? Oh, he must n't see me! Never, never, never! I made that promise to myself."

"Jane, you say yourself that you are changed, that you are not the girl he wants to find."

She shook her head desolately enough. "Oh, no, I'm not."

"He is n't sure that Jane West is the woman he's looking for. He's following the faintest, the most doubtful, of trails. He heard of you from

Yarnall; the description of you and your sudden flight made him fairly sure that it must be — you —" Jasper laughed. "I'm talking quite at random in a sense, because I have n't a notion, my dear, who you are nor what this Pierre has been in your life. If you could tell me — ?"

She shook her head. "No," she said; "no."

"Very well. Then I'll have to go on talking at random. Jane at the Lazy-Y Ranch was a woman who had deliberately disguised herself. Jane West in New York is a different woman altogether; but, unless I'm very wrong, she is even more completely disguised from Pierre Landis. If you can convince Pierre that you *are* Jane West, not any other woman, certainly not the woman he once knew, are n't you pretty safely rid of him for always?"

She stood still now. He felt that her fingers were cold. "Yes. For always. I suppose so. But how can I do that, Mr. Morena?"

"Nothing easier. You're an actress, are n't you? I advised Pierre Landis to stand near the stage exit to-night and watch you get into your motor."

Again she clutched at him. "Oh, no. Don't — don't let him do that!"

"Now, if you will make an effort, look him in

the eyes, refuse to show a single quiver of recognition, speak to some one in the most artificial tone you can manage, pass him by, and drive away, why, would n't that convince him that you are n't his quarry — eh?"

She thought! then slowly drew herself away and stood, her head bent, her brows drawn sharply together. "Yes. I suppose so. I think I can do it. That is the best plan." She looked at him wildly again. "Then it will be over for always, won't it? He'll go away?"

"Yes, my poor child. He will go away. He told me so. Then, will you try to forget him, to live your life for its own beautiful sake? I'd like to see you happy, Jane."

"Would you?" She smiled like a pitying mother. "Why, I've given up even dreaming of that. That is n't what keeps me going."

"What is it, then, Jane?"

"Oh, a queer notion." She laughed sadly. "A kind of kid's notion, I guess, that if you live along, some way, some time, you'll be able to make up for things you've done, and that perhaps there'll be another meeting-place — a kind of a round-up — where you'll be fit to forgive those you love and to be forgiven by them."

Jasper walked about. He was touched and

troubled. Some minutes later he said doubtfully, "Then you'll carry through your purpose of not letting Pierre know you?"

"Yes. I've made up my mind to that. That's what I've got to do. He must n't find me. We can't meet here in this life. That's certain. There are things that come between, things like bars." She made a strange gesture as of a prisoner running his fingers across the barred window of a cell. "Thank you for warning me. Thank you for telling me what to do." She smiled faintly. "I think he will know me, anyway," she said, "but I won't know him. Never! Never!"

That night the theater was late in emptying itself. Jane West had acted with especial brilliance and she was called out again and again. When she came to her dressing-room she was flushed and breathless. She did not change her costume, but drew her fur coat on over the green evening dress she had worn in the last scene. Then she stood before her mirror, looking herself over carefully, critically. Now that the paint was washed off, and the flush of excitement faded, she looked haggard and white. Her face was very thin, its beautiful bones — long sweep of jaw, wide brow, straight, short nose — sharply accentuated. The round throat rising against the fur collar looked unnaturally white and long. She sat down before her dressing-table and deliberately painted her cheeks and lips. She even altered the outlines of her mouth, giving it a pursed and doll-like expression, so that her eyes appeared enormous and her nose a little pinched. Then she drew a lock of waved hair down across the middle of her forehead, pressed another at each side close to the corners of her eyes. This took from the unusual breadth of brow and gave her a much more ordinary look. A coat of powder, heavily applied, more nearly produced the effect of a pink-and-white, glassy-eyed doll-baby for which she was trying. Afterwards she turned and smiled doubtfully at the astonished dresser.

"Good gracious, Miss West! You don't look like yourself at all!"

"Good!"

She said good-night and went rapidly down the draughty passages and the concrete stairs. Jasper was standing inside the outer door and applauded her.

"Well done. If it were n't for your pose and walk, my dear, I should hardly have known you myself."

Joan stood beside him, holding her furs close, breathing fast through the parted, painted lips.

"Is he here, do you know?"

"Yes. He's been waiting. I told him you might be late. Now, keep your head. Everything depends upon that. Can you do it?"

"Oh, yes. Is the car there? I won't have to stop?"

"Not an instant. But give him a good looking-over so that he'll be sure, and don't change the expression of your eyes. Feel, make yourself feel *inside*, that he's a stranger. You know what I mean. Good-night, my dear. Good luck. I'll call you up as soon as you get home — that is, after I've seen your pursuer safely back to his rooms." But this last sentence was addressed to himself.

Joan opened the door and stepped out into the chill dampness of the April night. The white arc of electric light beat down upon her as she came forward and it fell as glaringly upon the figure of Pierre. He had pushed forward from the little crowd of nondescripts always waiting at a stage exit, and stood, bareheaded, just at the door of her motor drawn up by the curb. She saw him instantly and from the first their eyes met. It was a horrible moment for Joan. What it was for him, she could tell by the tense pallor of his keen, bronzed face. The eyes she had not seen for such an agony of years, the strange, deep, iris-colored eyes, there they were now searching her. She stopped her heart in its beating, she stopped her breath, stopped her brain. She became for those few seconds just one thought — "I have never seen you. I have never seen you." She passed so close to him that her fur touched his hand, and she looked into his face with a cool, half-disdainful glitter of a smile.

"Step aside, please," she said; "I must get in." Her voice was unnaturally high and quite unnaturally precise.

Pierre said one word, a hopeless word. "Joan." It was a prayer. It should have been, "Be Joan." Then he stepped back and she stumbled into shelter.

At the same instant another man — a man in evening dress — hastily prevented her man from closing the door.

"Miss West, may I see you home?"

Before she could speak, could do more than look, Prosper Gael had jumped in, the door slammed, the car began its whirr, and they were gliding through the crowded, brilliant streets.

Joan had bent forward and was rocking to and fro.

"He called me 'Joan,'" she gasped over and over. "He called me 'Joan.'"

"That was Pierre?" Prosper had been forewarned by Jasper and had planned his part.

She kept on rocking, holding her hands on either side of her face.

"I must go away. If I see him again I shall die. I could never do that another time. O God! His hand touched me. He called me 'Joan' . . . I must go . . ."

Prosper did not touch her, but his voice, very friendly, very calm, had an instantaneous effect. "I will take you away."

She laughed shakily. "Again?" she asked, and shamed him into silence.

But after a while he began very reasonably, very patiently:

"I can take you away so that you need not be put through this unnecessary pain. I can arrange it with Morena. If Pierre sees you often enough, he will be sure to recognize you. Joan, I did not deserve that 'again' and you know it. I am a changed man. If you don't know that now I have the heart of — of devotion, of service, toward you, you are indeed a blind and stupid woman. But you do know it. You must."

She sat silent beside him, the long and slender hand between her face and him.

"I can take you away," he went on presently,

"and keep you from Pierre until he has given up his search and has gone West again. And I can take you at once — in a day or two. Your understudy can fill the part. This engagement is almost at an end. I can make it up to Morena. After all, if we go, we shall be doing Betty and him a service."

Joan flung out her hands recklessly. "Oh," she cried, "what does it matter? Of course I'll go. I'd run into the sea to escape Pierre —" She leaned back against the cushioned seat, rolled her head a little from side to side like a person in pain. "Take me away," she repeated. "I believe that if I stay I shall go mad. I'll go anywhere — with any one. Only take me away."

CHAPTER XII

THE LEOPARDESS

PIERRE stood before the cheap bureau of his ugly hotel bedroom turning a red slip of cardboard about in his fingers. The gas-jet sputtering above his head threw heavy shadows down on his face. It was the face of hopeless, heartsick youth, the muscles sagging, the eyes dull, the lips tight and pale. Since last night when the contemptuous glitter of Joan's smile had fallen upon him, he had neither slept nor eaten. Jasper had joined him at the theater exit, had walked home with him, and, while he was with the manager, Pierre's pride and reserve had held him up. Afterwards he had ranged the city like a prairie wolf, ranged it as though it had been an unpeopled desert, free to his stride. He had fixed his eyes above and beyond and walked alone in pain.

Dawn found him again in his room. What hope had sustained him, what memory of Joan, what purpose of tenderness toward her — these hopes and memories and purposes now choked and twisted him. He might have found her, his "gel," his Joan, with her dumb, loving gaze; he might have told her the story of his sorrow in such a way that she, who forgave so easily, would have forgiven even him, and he might have comforted her, holding her so and so, showing her utterly the true, unchanged, greatly changed love of his chastened heart. This girl, this love of his, whom, in his drunken, jealous madness, he had branded and driven away, he would have brought her back and tended her and made it up to her in a thousand, in ten thousand, ways. Pierre knelt by his bed, his black head buried in the cover, his arms bent above it, his hands clenched. Out there he had never lost hope of finding her, but here, in this peopled loneliness, with a memory of that woman's heartless smile, he did at last despair. In a strange, torturing way she had been like Joan. His heart had jumped to his mouth at first sight of her. And just there, to his shoulder where her head reached, had Joan's dear black head reached too. Pierre groaned aloud. The picture of her was so vivid. Not in months had the reality of his "gel" come so close to his imagination. He could feel her — feel her! O God!

That was the sort of night he had spent and the next day he passed in a lethargy. He had no heart to face the future now that the great purpose of his life had failed. Holliwell's God of comfort and forgiveness forsook him. What did he want with a God when that one comrade of his lonely, young, human life was out there lost by his own cruelty! Perhaps she was dead. Perhaps the wound had killed her. For all these years she might have been lying dead somewhere in the snow, under the sky. Sharp periods of pain followed dull periods of stupor. Now it was night again and a recollection of Jasper's theater ticket had dragged him to a vague purpose. He wanted to see again that woman who had so vivified his memory of Joan. It would be hateful to see her again, but he wanted the pain. He dressed and groomed himself carefully. Then, feeling a little faint, he went out into the clattering, glaring night.

Pierre's experience of theater-going was exceedingly small. He had never been in so large a play-house as this one of Morena's; he had never seen so large and well-dressed an audience; never heard a full and well-trained orchestra. In spite of himself, he began to be distracted, excited, stirred. When the curtain rose on the beautiful tropical scene, the lush island, the turquoise sea, the realistic strip of golden sand, Pierre gave an audible oath of admiration and surprise. The people about him began to be amused by the excitement of this handsome, haggard young man, so graceful and intense, so different with his hardness and leanness, the brilliance of his eyes, the brownness of his skin. His clothes were good enough, but they fitted him with an odd air of disguise. An experienced eye would inevitably have seen the appropriateness of flannel shirt, gay silk neck-handkerchief, boots, spurs, and *chaparreras*. Pierre was entirely unaware of being interesting or different. At that moment, caught up in the action of the play, he was as outside of himself as a child.

The palms of stage-land stirred, the ferns swayed; between their tall, vivid greenness came Joan with her tread and grace and watchful eyes of a leopardess, her loose, wild hair decked with flowers: these and her make-up and her thinness disguised her completely from Pierre, but again his heart came to his throat and, when she put her hands up to her mouth and called, his pulses gave a leap. He shut his eyes. He remembered a voice calling him in to supper. "Pi-erre! Pi-erre!" He could sniff the smoke of his cabin fire. He opened his eyes. Of course, she was n't Joan, this strange, gaunt creature. Besides, his wife could never have done what this woman was doing. Why, Joan could n't talk like this, she could n't act to save her soul! She was as simple as a child, and shy, with the unself-conscious shyness of wild things. To be sure, this "actress-lady" was making-believe she was a wild thing, and she was doing it almighty well, but Joan had been the reality, and grave and still, part of his own big, grave, mountain country, not a fierce, man-devouring animal of the tropics. Pierre lived in the play with all but one fragment of his brain, and that remembered Joan. It hurt like a hot coal, but he deliberately ignored the pain of it. He followed the action breathlessly, applauded with contagious fervor, surreptitiously rid himself of tears, and when, in the last scene, the angry, jealous woman sprang upon her tamer, he muttered, "Serve you right, you coyote!" with an oath of the cow-camp that made one of his neighbors jump and throttle a startled laugh.

The curtain fell, and while the applause rose and died down and rose again, and the people called for "Jane West! Jane West!" the stage-director, a plump little Jew, came out behind the footlights and held up his hand. There was a gradual silence.

"I want to make an interesting announcement," he said; "the author of 'The Leopardess' has hitherto maintained his anonymity, but to-night I have permission to give you his name. He is in the theater to-night. The name is already familiar to you as that of the author of a popular novel, 'The Cañon': Prosper Gael."

There was a stir of interest, a general searching of the house, clapping, cries of "Author! Author!' and in a few moments Prosper Gael left his box and appeared beside the director in answer to the calls. He was entirely self-possessed, looked even a little bored, but he was very white. He stood there bowing, a graceful and attractive figure, and he was about to begin a speech when he was interrupted by a renewed calling for "Jane West!" The audience wanted to see the star and the author side by side. Pierre joined in the clamor.

After a little pause Jane West came out from the opposite wing, walking slowly, dressed in her green gown, jewels on her neck and in her hair. She did not look toward the audience at all, nor bow, nor smile, and for some reason the applause began to falter as though the sensitive mind of the crowd was already aware that here something must be wrong. She came very slowly, her arms hanging, her head bent, her eyes looking up from under her brows, and she stood beside Prosper Gael, whose forced smile had stiffened on his lips. He looked at her in obvious fear, as a man might look at a dangerous madwoman. There must have been madness in her eyes. She stood there for a strange, terrible moment, moving her head slightly from side to side. Then she said something in a very low tone. Because of the extraordinary carrying quality of her voice — the question was heard by every one there present:

"*You* wrote the play? *You* wrote the play?"

She said it twice. She seemed to quiver, to gather herself together, her hands bent, her arms lifted. She flew at Prosper with all the sudden strength of her insanity.

There was an outcry, a confusion. People rushed to Gael's assistance. Men caught hold of Joan, now struggling frantically. It was a dreadful sight, mercifully a brief one. She collapsed utterly, fell forward, the strap of her gown breaking in the grasp of one of the men who held her. For an instant every one in the audience saw a strange double scar that ran across her shoulder to the edge of the shoulder-blade. It was like two bars.

Pierre got to his feet, dropped back, and hid

his face. Then he was up, and struggling past excited people down the row, out into the aisle, along it, hurrying blindly down unknown passages till somehow he got himself into that confused labyrinth behind the scenes. Here a pale, distracted scene-shifter informed him that Miss West had already been taken home.

Pierre got the address, found his way out to the street, hailed a taxicab, and threw himself into it. He sat forward, every muscle tight; he felt that he could take the taxicab up and hurl it forward, so terrible was his impatience.

An apartment house was a greater novelty to him even than a theater, but, after a dazed moment of discovering that he did not have to ring or knock, but just push open the great iron-scrolled door and step into the brightly lighted, steam-heated marble hall, he decided that the woman at the desk was a person in authority, and to her he addressed himself, soft hat gripped in his hand, his face set to hide excitement.

The girl was pale and red-eyed. They had brought Miss West in a few minutes ago, she told him, and carried her up. She was still unconscious; poor thing! "I don't think you could see her, sir. Mr. Morena is up there, and Mr. Gael, and a doctor. A trained nurse has been sent for. Everything in the world will be done. She's such an elegant actress, ain't she? I've often seen her myself. And so kind and pleasant always. Yes, sir. I'll ask, if you like, but I'm sure they won't allow you up."

She put the receiver to her ear, pushed in the black plug, and Pierre listened to her questions.

"Can Miss West see any one? Can an old friend" — for so Pierre had named himself — "be allowed to see her? No. I thought not." This, with a sympathetic glance at Pierre. "She is not conscious yet. Dangerously ill."

"Could I speak to the doctor?" Pierre asked hoarsely.

"The gentleman wants to know if he can speak to the doctor. Certainly not at present. If he will wait, the doctor will speak to him on the way out."

Pierre sat on the bench and waited. He leaned forward, elbows on knees, head crushed in both hands, and the woman stared at him pitilessly — not that he was aware of her scrutiny. His eyes looked through his surroundings to Joan. He saw her in every pose and in every look in which he had ever seen her, and, with a very sick and frightened heart, he saw her, at the last, pass by him in her fur coat, throwing him that half-contemptuous look and smile. She did n't know him. Was he changed so greatly? Or was the change in her so enormous that it had disassociated her completely from her old life, from him? He kept repeating to himself Holliwell's stern, admonishing speech: "However changed for the worse she may be when you do find her, Pierre, you must remember that it is your fault, your sin. You must not judge her, must not dare to judge her. Judge yourself. Condemn yourself. It is for her to forgive if she can bring herself to do it."

So now Pierre fought down his suspicions and his fears. He had not recognized Prosper. The man who had come in out of the white night, four years ago, had worn his cap low over his eyes, his collar turned up about his face, and, even at that, Pierre, in his drunken stupor, had not been able to see him very clearly. This Prosper Gael who had stood behind the footlights, this Prosper Gael at whom Joan, from some unknown cause, had sprung like a woman maddened by injury, was a person entirely strange to Pierre. But Pierre hated him. The man had done Joan some insufferable mischief, which at the last had driven her beside herself. Pierre put up a hand, pressing it against his eyes. He wanted to shut out the picture of that struggling girl with her torn dress and the double scar across her shoulder. If it had n't been for the scar he would never have known her — his Joan, his gentle, silent Joan! What had they been doing to her to change her so? No, not they. He. He had changed her. He had branded her and driven her out. It was his fault. He must try to find her again, to find the old Joan — if she should live. The doctor had said that she was desperately ill. O God! What was keeping him so long? Why did n't he come?

The arrival of the trained nurse distracted Pierre for a few moments. She went past him in her gray cloak, very quiet and earnest, and the elevator lifted her out of sight.

"Were you in the theater to-night?" asked the girl at the desk, seeing that he was temporarily aware of her again.

"Yes, ma'am."

She was puzzled by his appearance and the fashion of his speech. He must be a gentleman, she thought, for his bearing was gentle and assured and unself-conscious, but he wore his clothes differently and spoke differently from other gentlemen. That "Yes, ma'am," especially disturbed her. Then she remembered a novel she had read and her mind jumped to a conclusion. She leaned forward.

"Say, are n't you from the West?"

"Yes, ma'am."

"You were n't ever a cowboy, were you?"

Pierre smiled. "Yes, ma'am. I was raised in a cow-camp. I was a cowboy till about seven years ago when I took to ranchin'."

"Where was that?"

"Out in Wyoming."

"And you 've come straight from there to New York?" She pronounced it "Noo Yoik."

"No, ma'am. I 've been in Alasky for two years now. I 've been in a lumber-camp."

"Gee! That 's real interesting. And you knew Miss West before she came East, then?"

"Yes, ma'am." But there was a subtle change in Pierre's patient voice and clear, unhappy eyes, so that the girl fell to humming and bottled up her curiosity. But just as soon as he began to brood again she gave up her whole mind to staring at him. Gee! He was brown and strong and thin! And a good-looker! She wished that she had worn her transformation that evening and her blue blouse. He might have taken more interest in her.

A stout, bald-headed man, bag in hand, stepped out of the elevator, and Pierre rippled to his feet.

"Are you the doctor?"

"Yes. Oh, you 're the gentleman who wanted

to see Miss West. She's come to, but she is out of her head completely . . . does n't know any one. Can you step out with me?"

Pierre kept beside him and stood by the motor, hat still in his hand, while the doctor talked irritably: "No. You certainly can't see her, for some time. I shall not allow any one to see her, except the nurse. It will be a matter of weeks. She'll be lucky if she gets back her sanity at all. She was entirely out of her head there at the theater. She's worn out, nerves frayed to a frazzle. Horribly unhealthy life and unnatural. To take a country girl, an ignorant, untrained, healthy animal, bring her to the city and force her under terrific pressure into a life so foreign to her — well! it was just a piece of d——d brutality." Then his acute eye suddenly fixed itself on the man standing on the curb listening.

"You're from the West yourself?"

"Yes, sir."

"Knew her in the old days — eh?"

"Yes, sir." Pierre's voice was faint and he put a hand against the motor.

"Well, why don't you take her back with you to that life? You're not feeling any too fit yourself, are you? Look here. Get in and I'll drop you where you belong."

Pierre obeyed rather blindly and leaned back with closed eyes. The doctor got out a flask and poured him a dose of brandy.

"What's the trouble? Too much New York?"

Pierre shook his head and smiled. "No, sir. I've been bothered and did n't get round to eating and sleeping lately."

"Then I'll take you to a restaurant and we'll have supper. I need something myself. And, look here, I'll make you a promise. Just as soon as I consider her fit for an interview with any one, I'll let you see Miss West. That helps you a whole lot, does n't it?"

But there were other powers, besides this friendly one, watching over Joan, and they were bent upon keeping Pierre away. Day after sickening day Pierre came and stood beside the desk, and the girl, each time a little more careless of him, a little more insolent toward him — for the cowboy would not notice her blue blouse and her transformation and the invitation of her eyes — gave him negligent and discouraging information.

"Miss West was better, but very weak. No. She would n't see any one. Yes, Mr. Morena could see her, but not Mr. Landis, certainly not Mr. Pierre Landis, of Wyoming."

And the doctor, being questioned by the half-frantic Westerner, admitted that Mr. Morena had hinted at reasons why it might be dangerous for the patient to see her old friend from the West. Pierre stood to receive this sentence, and after it, his eyes fell. The doctor had seen the quick, desperate moisture in them.

"I tell you what, Landis," he said, putting a hand on Pierre's shoulder. "I'm willing to take a risk. I'm sure of one thing. Miss West has n't even heard of your inquiries."

"You mean Morena's making it up — about her not being willing to see me?"

"I do mean that. And no doubt he's doing it with the best intentions. But I'm willing to take a risk. See those stairs? You run up them to the fifth floor. The nurse is out. Gael is in attendance; that is, he's in the sitting-room. She does n't know of his presence, has n't been allowed to see him. Miss West's door — the outside one — is ajar. Go up. Get past Gael if you can. Behave yourself quietly, and if you see the least sign of weakness on the part of Miss West, or if she shows the slightest disinclination for your company, come down — I'm trusting you — as quickly as you can and tell me. I'll wait. Have I your promise?"

"Yes, sir," gasped Pierre.

The doctor smiled at the swift, leaping grace of his Western friend's ascent. He was anxious concerning the result of his experiment, but there was a memory upon him of a haunted look in Joan's eyes that seemed the fellow to a look of Pierre's. He rather believed in intuitions, especially his own.

CHAPTER XIII

THE END OF THE TRAIL

AT the top of the fourth flight of steps, Pierre found himself facing a door that stood ajar. Beyond that door was Joan and he knew not what experience of discovery, of explanation, of punishment. What he had suffered since the night of his cruelty would be nothing to what he might have to suffer now at the hands of the woman he had loved and hurt. That she was incredibly changed he knew, what had happened to change her he did not know. That she had suffered greatly was certain. One could not look at the face of Jane West, even under its disguise of paint and pencil, without a sharp realization of profound and embittering experience. And, just as certainly, she had gone far ahead of her husband in learning, in a certain sort of mental and social development. Pierre was filled with doubt and with dread, with an almost unbearable self-depreciation. And at the same time he was filled with a nameless fear of what Joan might herself have become.

He stood with his hand on the knob of that

half-opened door, bent his head, and drew some deep, uneven breaths. He thought of Holliwell as though the man were standing beside him. He stepped in quietly, shut the door, and walked without hesitation down the passageway into the little, sunny sitting-room. There, before the crackling, open fire, sat Prosper Gael.

Prosper, it seemed, was alone in the small, silent place. He was sitting on the middle of his spine, as usual, with his long, thin legs stretched out before him and a veil of cigarette smoke before his eyes. He turned his head idly, expecting, no doubt, to see the nurse.

Pierre, white and grim, stood looking down at him.

The older man recognized him at once, but he did not change his position by a muscle, merely lounged there, his head against the side of the cushioned chair, the brilliant, surprised gaze changing slowly to amused contempt. His cigarette hung between the long fingers of one hand, its blue spiral of smoke rising tranquilly into a bar of sunshine from the window.

"The doctor told me to come up," said Pierre gravely. He was aware of the insult of this stranger's attitude, but he was too deeply stirred, too deeply suspenseful, to be irritated by it. He seemed to be moving in some rare, disconnected atmosphere. "I have his permission to see — to see Miss West, if she is willing to see me."

Prosper flicked off an ash with his little finger. "And you believe that she is willing to see you, Pierre Landis?" he asked slowly.

Pierre gave him a startled look. "You know my name?"

"Yes. I believe that four years ago, on an especially cold and snowy night, I interrupted you in a rather extraordinary occupation and gave myself the pleasure of shooting you." With that he got to his feet and stood before the mantel, negligently enough, but ready to his finger-tips.

Pierre came nearer by a stride. He had been stripped at once of his air of high detachment. He was pale and quivering. He looked at Prosper with eyes of incredulous dread.

"Were you — that man?" A tide of shamed scarlet engulfed him and he dropped his eyes.

"I thought that would take the assurance out of you," said Prosper. "As a matter of fact, shooting was too good for you. On that night you forfeited every claim to the consideration of man or woman. I have the right of any decent citizen to turn you out of here. Do you still maintain your intention of asking for an interview with Miss Jane West?"

Pierre, half-blind with humiliation, turned without a word and made his way to the door. He meant to go away and kill himself. The purpose was like iron in his mind. That he should have to stand and, because of his own cowardly fault, to endure insult from this contemptuous stranger, made of life a garment too stained, too shameful to be worn. He was in haste to be rid of it. Something, however, barred his exit. He stumbled back to avoid it. There, holding aside the curtain in the doorway, stood Joan.

This time there was no possible doubt of her identity. She was wrapped in a long, blue gown, her hair had fallen in braided loops on either side of her face and neck. The unchanged eyes of Joan under her broad brows looked up at him. She was thin and wan, unbelievably broken and tired and hurt, but she was Joan. Pierre could not but forget death at sight of her. He staggered forward, and she, putting up her arms, drew him hungrily and let fall her head upon his shoulder.

"My gel! My Joan!" Pierre sobbed.

Prosper's voice sawed into their tremulous silence.

"So, after all, the branding iron is the proper

instrument," he said. "A man can always recognize his estray, and when she is recognized she will come to heel."

Joan pushed Pierre from her violently and turned upon Prosper Gael. Her voice broke over him in a tumult of soft scorn.

"You know nothing of loving, Prosper Gael, not the first letter of loving. Nobody has learned that about you as well as I have. Now, listen and I will teach you something. This is something that *I* have learned. There are worse wounds than I had from Pierre, and it is by the hands of such men as you are that they are given. The hurts you get from love, they heal. Pierre was mad, he was a beast, he branded me as though I had been a beast. For long years I could n't think of him but with a sort of horror in my heart. If it had n't been for you, I might never have thought of him no other way forever. But what you did to me, Prosper, you with your white-hot brain and your gray-cold heart, you with your music and your talk throbbing and talking and whining about my soul, what you did to me has made Pierre's iron a very gentle thing. I have not acted in the play you wrote, the play you made out of me and my unhappiness, without understanding just what it was that you did to me. Perhaps if it had n't been for the play, I might even have believed that you were capable of something better than that passion you had once for me — but not now. Never now can I believe it. What you make other people suffer is material for your own success and you delight in it. You make notes upon it. Pierre was mad through loving me, too ignorantly, too jealously, but what you did to me was through loving me too little. That was a brand upon my brain and soul. Sometimes since then that scar on my shoulder has seemed to me almost like the memory of a caress. I went away from Pierre, leaving him for dead, ready for death myself. When you left me, you left me alive and ready for what sort of living? It has been Pierre's love and his following after me that have kept me from low and beastly things. I've run from him knowing I was n't fit to be found by him, but I've run clean and free." She began to tremble. "Will you say anything more to me and to my man?"

Prosper's face wore its old look of the winged demon. He was cold in his angry pain.

"Just one thing to your man, perhaps, if you will allow me, but perhaps you'll tell him that yourself. That his method is the right one, I admit. But in one respect not even a brand will altogether preserve property rights. Morena could say something on that score. So could I . . ."

"Hush!" said Joan; "I will tell him myself. Pierre, I left you for dead and I went away with this man, and after a while, because I thought you were dead, and because I was alone and sorrowful and weak, and because, perhaps, of what my mother was, I — I —" She fell away from Pierre, crouched against the side of the door, and wrapped the curtain round her face. "He told me you were dead —" The words came muffled.

Pierre had let her go and turned to Prosper. His own face was a mask of rage. Prosper knew that it was the Westerner's intention to kill. For a minute, no longer, he was a lightning channel of death. But Pierre, the Pierre shaped during the last four difficult years, turned upon his own writhing, savage soul and forced it to submit. It was as though he fought with his hands. Sweat broke out on him. At last, he stood and looked at Prosper with sane, stern eyes.

"If that's true what you hinted, if that's true what she was tryin' to tell, if it's even partly true," he said painfully, "then it was me that brought it upon her, not you — an' not herself, but me."

He turned back to Joan, drew the curtain

from her face, drew down her hands, lifted her and carried her to the couch beside the fire.

There she shrank away from him, tried to push him back.

"It's true, Pierre; not that about Morena, but the rest is true. It's true. Only he told me you were dead. But you were n't — no, don't take my hands. I never did have dealings with Holliwell. Indeed, I loved only you. But you must have known me better than I knew myself. For I am bad. I am bad. I left you for dead and I went away."

He had mastered her hands, both of them in one of his, and he drew them close to his heart.

"Don't Joan! Hush, Joan! You must n't. It was my doings, gel, all of it. Hush!"

He bent and crushed his lips against hers, silencing her. Then she gave way and clung to him, sobbing.

After a while Pierre looked up at Prosper Gael. All the patience and the hunger and the beauty of his love possessed his face. There was simply no room in his heart for any lesser thing.

"Stranger," he said in the grave and gentle Western speech, "I'll have to ask you to leave me with my wife."

Prosper made a curious, silent gesture of self-despair and went out, feeling his way before him.

It was half an hour later when the doctor came softly to the door and held back the curtain in his hand. He did not say anything and, after a silent minute, he let fall the curtain and moved softly away. He was reassured as to the success of his experiment. He had seen Joan's face.

THE END

www.ingramcontent.com/pod-product-compliance
Lightning Source LLC
LaVergne TN
LVHW030908080826
845145LV00010B/2816

9781410100832